MODERN BRAZILIAN SHORT STORIES

MODERN
BRAZILIAN
SHORT STORIES

Translated with an Introduction by
WILLIAM L. GROSSMAN

* *
*

UNIVERSITY OF CALIFORNIA PRESS
Berkeley and Los Angeles 1967

The English translation of
"The Crime of the Mathematics Professor" and "Guidance" originally appeared in the December 1961 issue of *Odyssey Review,* Copyright © 1961 by the Latin American and European Literary Society, Incorporated. Grateful acknowledgment is made to Penguin Books, Ltd., for permission to publish an English translation of Vasconcelos Maia's "Sol."

University of California Press
Berkeley and Los Angeles, California
Cambridge University Press
London, England

Published with the assistance of a grant
from the Rockefeller Foundation
Library of Congress Catalog Card Number: 67–13379
Printed in the United States of America

Acknowledgments

I owe an immense debt to Dora Vasconcellos and to Leo Peracchi, each of whom expertly and painstakingly helped me to understand the precise meaning of the text of certain of the stories.

The English version of "The Crime of the Mathematics Professor" was produced jointly by José Roberto Vasconcellos and myself.

In connection with the introduction, I am grateful to Wilson Martins for observations based on his profound knowledge and understanding of modern Brazilian literature.

W. L. G.

Contents

Translator's Introduction

The modernist movement, which dominated Brazilian literature from 1922 to 1945, intensified the effort or tendency of writers to become genuinely Brazilian in idiom, in spirit, and in subject matter. Earlier writers in general were charged with having composed academic or Lusitanian Portuguese rather than Brazilian Portuguese and, what was worse, with having been indifferent to the national reality. "If our customs and our landscapes were captured," says the fictionist Renard Perez, "our essence was not. The Brazilian soul remained unexplored." [1]

The modernists, then, sought to write authentically as Brazilians about Brazil. In the short story, according to Perez, the principal exponents of this tendency were Mário de Andrade, Antônio de Alcântara Machado, and Ribeiro Couto. All three are represented in the present collection. Indeed, almost all the authors of these stories—all, one might say, except Clarice Lispector—manifest in varying degree the nationalistic tendency of modernism. This is true even of Guimarães Rosa, the giant of post-modernist Brazilian fiction.

But, in Brazilian literature as in Brazilian political sentiment, nationalism is an elusive concept. Brazil is a vast and varied nation, and *minha terra*—my homeland, my native land—may mean one's own region rather than the entire country. Mário de Andrade and Alcântara Machado wrote about people in São Paulo; Darcy Azambuja writes about the far south; Marques Rebêlo writes about *cariocas,* especially in suburban Rio; Magalhães Júnior's story (among others) in this anthology takes place in the northeast, an especially fruitful setting of great fiction. All these authors, of course, are writing about Brazil. But is it the

---

[1] "A Evolução do Conto no Brasil," *Revista do Livro,* No. 19 (Sept. 1960), p. 69.

same Brazil? To what extent do their stories and the other stories here collected present a common spiritual or social reality? The reader must answer this question for himself, and his answer may reflect not only his perceptivity but also the extent to which there exists in fact a national Brazilian ethos. Quite possibly he will find greater similarity among the authors in their respective attitudes, in their ways of seeing and understanding, than in the aspects of Brazil or of Brazilians that they present in their stories. But the authors, too, are Brazilians, and, so far as they see alike, they may represent a common Brazilian way of seeing.

Especially striking is the irony in most of these stories. It is by no means fortuitous that Brazil's greatest man of letters, Machado de Assis (1839–1908), was also her supreme ironist. Many Brazilian writers are uncompromisingly insistent on revealing the naked spiritual reality of their characters and of the society in which those characters move. To such revelations the responsive author is likely to react with revulsion and anger or, what makes for better literature, with sarcasm, which, when sufficiently arch or when apparently implied by the narrative itself, may be called irony. For a lively example of this irony, I suggest the epistolatory study of parental concern, "With God's Blessing, Mom." The fact that this story won its author a prize would have little significance in a country where literary prizes abound, were it not that, as one of the judges, the renowned Graciliano Ramos (represented in this collection) voted for the story and wrote a vigorous defense of his choice. Brazilian fictionists sometimes achieve also the classical irony of the contrast between man's proposals and God's or fate's disposals, as in the exquisitely formed miniature, "Gaetaninho."

Death comes into most of these stories. And there is, in many of them, a pervasive melancholy, varying in tone from author to author. In several it appears to be, at least in part, the "Brazilian sadness" of which Paulo Prado (1869–1943) wrote in his celebrated book, *Retrato do Brasil* (*Portrait of Brazil*). "In a radiant land," said Prado, "lives a sad people." [2] Its melancholy, he explained, is an inevitable consequence of the traditions of greed and unbridled sensuality bequeathed by the early settlers of the country and not counterbalanced by a religious or aesthetic ideal

---

[2] 5th ed. (São Paulo: Editôra Brasiliense, 1944), p. 11.

or by devotion to political, intellectual, or artistic goals. Prado's compatriots differ in the extent to which they accept his theory. In any case, Brazilian writers also exploit other causes of sadness, such as poverty and interpersonal indifference; witness, notably, Mário de Andrade's touching story of a child, "It Can Hurt Plenty."

Brazilian writers are often at their best in stories about children. The inclusion of three such stories in the present collection reflects this fact, for which I have no firm explanation. Attention may be directed particularly to Marques Rebêlo, who is noted for his ability to capture the lyricism of childhood. "The Beautiful Rabbits" reveals this ability but shows that he can also suggest the desperation and cruelty of childhood.

I once asked a Brazilian diplomat, himself an author, whether there was not some fundamental Brazilian characteristic that defied geographical and social differences, something that the people as a whole had in common. He replied without hesitation that there was such a characteristic: an intense and mystical religious feeling. This is a very different answer from Paulo Prado's. If my diplomat is right, or even if he somewhat exaggerated the generality of the feeling among his countrymen, many Brazilian writers have apparently permitted their own positivistic outlook to blind them to an important element in Brazilian reality. Religion comes into two or three of these stories but constitutes a major element in only one of them, "The Enchanted Ox." Incidentally, this powerful apologue is ostensibly a children's story; I have taken the liberty of deleting the short passages concerning the fictitious narrator and the children to whom the story is being told.

This brief inventory does not begin to exhaust the varied substance of our little collection, much less of the Brazilian short story in general. Thus, in "My Father's Hat" and "At the Side of the Road" there is melancholy but there is also great personal warmth. Of the author of the former, Aurélio Buarque de Holanda, a Brazilian critic has written: "To his very pure and expressive language is joined the humanity of a loving observer, permanently poring over the great little things of daily life." [3]

---

[3] José Paulo Paes in *Maravilhas do Conto Moderno Brasileiro* (São Paulo: Editôra Cultrix, 1958), p. 170.

And there is humor in abundance: the mordant humor of "With God's Blessing, Mom," the wry yet hilarious humor of "The Piano," the casual humor of "Metonymy, or the Husband's Revenge," the almost Chaplinesque humor of "The Thief," and, one might add, the nostalgic humor of "My Father's Hat." Mário de Andrade was one of the founders of Brazilian modernism and became by far its most influential figure. His pronouncements therefore help one understand the major orientation of Brazilian literature during and even after the modernist period. He was, significantly, very critical of excessive or misdirected nationalism. "Our traditionalism," he wrote in 1923, "shall be principally human and universal." [4] And in praise of Alcântara Machado, author of "Gaetaninho," he said that although this writer's work was linked to São Paulo, "he has achieved, more and more, a strong universality. His characters are like the voices of good singers: they carry over a distance." [5] The ideal indicated by such statements, together with the humanistic sense of balance of Brazil's best writers, has prevented the nationalistic tendency from getting, or at least from long remaining, out of hand.

Even when the "local color" is striking, the most representative modern Brazilian fiction is almost never merely provincial or parochial. I think the stories in the present collection illustrate this point. The stuff of which they are made—and we have reviewed some of it—is the stuff of universal experience; only the proportions and modes of manifestation vary. Moreover, the authors of these stories avoid even the suggestion of chauvinism, and when their settings are provincial it is because the provinces are where they can see the universal comedy most vividly, most poignantly. In purporting to give us Brazilian reality, then, they have given us human reality with a Brazilian emphasis, a Brazilian feeling, a Brazilian application.

We non-Brazilians may consequently find the journey on which these authors invite us doubly rewarding. We are diverted

[4] *Revista do Brasil,* August 1923, quoted in Wilson Martins, *O Modernismo,* Vol. VI of *A Literatura Brasileira* (São Paulo: Editôra Cultrix, 1965), p. 75.
[5] Quoted on the cover of Antônio de Alcântara Machado, *Novelas Paulistanas* (Rio de Janeiro: Livraria José Olympio Editôra, 1961).

by the novelty and fascination of a foreign environment while being conducted, skillfully and unerringly, to the country where all of us, Brazilians and non-Brazilians, are equally at home; for there we can discover, stripped of nonessentials, ourselves—disguised as the frustrated fat man in "Sun," as the loving, selfish boy in "The Beautiful Rabbits," as the knavish backlander in "The Immunizer," as the moralistic family counselor in "Guidance," but always, to our delight and dismay, recognizably and undeniably ourselves.

WILLIAM L. GROSSMAN

R. Magalhães Júnior

The Immunizer

The lowland extended, broad and level, from Carnotim Range to the Jaibara River. Only the termite mounds interrupted its flatness. It was an enormous picture of desolation. The lowing of the oxen sounded like a death rattle as they gnawed at the remaining grass roots. The grass itself had been pitilessly scorched by the drought and then swept away by the fury of the whirlwinds. Indeed, virtually all the vegetation had disappeared. In the distance one could see the lone, spectral figure of a leafless tree on whose branches a flock of black vultures had settled, lending a note of mourning to the countryside.

In the midst of the plain, the sole survivor of the tragedy, a jujube tree spread its green, hospitable foliage over the exhausted traveler. The drought had transformed the fertile, generous backlands into a great Sahara, and the tree was a tiny oasis. It was here that Pedro Macambira * rested, setting down his cans of creosote around the ancient tree trunk. He had brought them to cure the mange sores from which several of the cattle were suffering. . . . They all should have been withdrawn from the area some time earlier. But the owner remained obstinate, although Saint Anthony's Day, then Saint John's Day, and finally Saint Peter's Day had come and gone without a drop of rain. He kept saying that, so long as the leaves of the jujube tree did not fall, there was still a good chance of rain, God willing. And so, every day, he put off the withdrawal of the cattle in the hope that the so-called winter weather would begin and everything would bud and sprout again. Meanwhile, the famished animals could hardly stay on their feet.

---

* Macambira is a variety of bromelia found in northeastern Brazil.

Macambira climbed the jujube tree and, from his improvised lookout, ran his eyes over the plain. Two more young steers had died and were serving as a repast for the hawks and vultures. The hawks, finicky gourmets that they are, ate only the eyes and then left the banquet.

The backlander's attention was diverted to something closer. Under the tree the old cow horse, Shooting Star, was snorting in great distress. With goggling eyes it appealed to him for help. The backlander's expert glance immediately discovered, right in front of the animal, the sinister coil of a rattlesnake, its fangs all set for the fatal thrust.

Macambira tore pieces of branches from the tree and threw them at the snake. In vain. With the swiftness of an arrow the snake buried its sharp fangs in the horse's leg. Shooting Star let out a horrible whinny. A thread of blood ran from its panting nostrils. Its knees buckled and the animal rolled on the ground, writhing and kicking. . . .

Lightning, the backlander's thin, shabby dog, whose main job was to bring back stray lambs, approached apprehensively and began to lick the body of its old companion. Through the years, they had worked together on so many roundups.

Fearful for the dog, Macambira scolded:

"Hey, get out of there, you mangy devil! Come here! You want the snake to bite you?"

And, as the dog paid no attention:

"I might just as well save my breath. . . . Here, Lightning, come here!"

The snake rattled. Lightning began to bark and move around it, trying to bring it to bay. The snake coiled again and attacked the skinny dog. Wounded on the muzzle, Lightning howled, curled into a ball, and rolled on the sandy ground like an armadillo.

The backlander thought that this faithful animal would die too. But, to his surprise, the dog got up and started to bark again, wagging its tail energetically. Macambira rejoiced. And he wondered why the sting of the snake had killed the horse and not the dog. His somewhat rudimentary deductive power was aided by the vague remembrance of a story he had heard, many

years before, about poisonous snakes. Yes, that must be it. The
snake had almost exhausted its supply of poison on the horse,
and what was left had been insufficient to kill the dog.

Then an ingenious plan of fraud and deceit began to take
form in his mind. He came down from the tree and resolutely
grabbed the snake in his hands. Despite repeated thrusts of the
snake's fangs, he shut it up in the calabash in which he had
brought his ration of muddy, salty water from the ranch.

The leaves of the jujube tree did not fall. The rain came at
last, plentifully, and watered the scorched earth. Before long,
that desolate landscape was miraculously transformed. Thick,
green, luxuriant vegetation covered the low plains and the scrub
lands. And the heroic backlanders felt the breath of renewed
faith.

Pedro Macambira, too, had passed through a radical metamorphosis. Now he called himself Pedro the Healer. A halo of
mystery hovered over him. It was whispered that he had magic
powers, that he was possessed. He could protect people against
snakes; he could take any Christian and make him completely
immune to the sting of these accursed creatures.

Macambira said little. He had assumed a priestly manner and
had let his beard grow wild. The prophet in the wilderness who
ate grasshoppers must have looked very much like him. His fame
spread from Palma to Tamboril, from Cariré to Araticum. He
went with his rattlesnake to all the market fairs and, to demon-
strate his peculiar power, let it bite him. Then, for everyone who
wanted to buy similar immunity, he would say a prayer against
snakes. He proved its effectiveness by having the person expose
an arm and get bitten by the rattlesnake, with no ill effect.

The trick was infallible and the compensation abundant. Pedro
Macambira amassed a fortune, almost enough to buy a small
farm in the Serra Grande where he could plant corn and cassava.

After a long time he returned to the ranch, a bit fearful that
his old companions would question his supernatural gift. There
he found the ranch owner's son, just back from medical school
in Bahia and now a full-fledged doctor. The two had been childhood playmates, with their rawhide whips always in hand, killing
birds, stealing nests . . .

Dr. Griljava was interested in Pedro Macambira's witchcraft, and the backlander told him everything, as on old friend should. He had observed that a rattlesnake kills only with the first bite. So all he had to do was go to the marshes during the night and catch frogs. Early in the morning he would get the snake angry and throw the frogs in the calabash. "Enjoy yourself!" And then he could take the rattlesnake in his hand as if it were a tame little bird.

The doctor laughed loud and long. And he laughed again when Macambira complained that the worst part of it was going to the swamps every night to catch frogs, with the danger of running into poisonous snakes there.

Dr. Griljava offered to relieve his friend of such an arduous task by extracting the snake's poison glands. The snake would then be as harmless as an earthworm. The backlander eagerly agreed. And henceforth he continued his career as an immunizer without the worry and nuisance of having to beat the marshes, torch in hand, in search of those miserable frogs.

One day Pedro Macambira left the market fair at Palma and took the road across Pajeú [Sandgrass] Plateau to Mucambo. The famous immunizer stopped on the bank of the Ema River to rest and to appease his hunger with roast meat and a bar of brown sugar. He dismounted, took his horse to the river, and, in compensation for its long day's work, bathed it. He did not notice that the pressure of the saddle had split the calabash down the middle and that the snake, taking advantage of this happy opportunity, had made the escape it had perhaps long dreamed of. . . .

Back from the river, Macambira ate unconcernedly. Then, as he was about to saddle the horse, he noticed the split calabash and understood that his breadwinner, his treasure, had ungratefully fled his company. Alarmed and agitated, he hastily tied his horse to a tree and followed the thin, sinuous trail across the fine sand of the plateau. The trail could be clearly seen, for there was almost no vegetation. He felt sure he would find the snake. Wasn't he, Macambira, the best tracker in that part of the country!

Farther on, however, the backlander had an unhappy surprise.

Directly ahead of him lay an enormous bed of flat rock. It extended more than ten meters. On the black, brutal stone, the snake's trail disappeared. Macambira almost decided to give up. But he thought of the fair at Mucambo, attended by all the rich ranchers of the region. He could earn at least two hundred milreis. So he resumed the search. He walked around the edge of the rock bed, looking for the resumption of the trail. After a long, minute search, he let out a cry of joy.

There it was again, the thin line traced in the sand. He followed it. Ahead, near a cactus, he saw a small, gray coil. "At last," thought the backlander. He advanced and extended his arm. The rattlesnake thrust at him and buried its fangs in the back of his hand. Macambira tried to pick up the snake, but he could not. His arm felt heavy as lead. A wave of blood rushed to his head and spilled out at his lips, his nostrils, his eyes.

And frothing at the mouth, howling, gnashing his teeth in agony, the backlander fell to the ground. He panted for almost an hour, at first like a bellows and then more and more gently, until he stiffened in a tragic posture of finality.

RAIMUNDO MAGALHÃES JÚNIOR was born in 1907 in Ubajara in the northeastern state of Ceará. At the age of sixteen he moved southward, ultimately settling in Rio de Janeiro, where he still lives. He has distinguished himself in diversified literary activities, including journalism, fiction, biography, history, and the preparation of anthologies. From time to time he writes poems, one of which appeared in translation in *New Directions*. His essays on Machado de Assis comprise three volumes, and he has organized several books of previously uncollected works by this Brazilian master. He is one of Brazil's most successful playwrights. He edits the magazine *Manchete*. In 1956 he was elected to membership in the Brazilian Academy of Letters.

Magalhães Júnior came to New York in 1940 as correspondent of the newspaper *A Noite*. He remained eight months, working also as a film translator for M.G.M. and as press agent for the Brazilian pavilion at the World's Fair. He returned to New York in 1942 as special assistant in the Brazilian section of the office of the Coordinator of Inter-American Affairs (Nelson Rockefeller). This time he remained two years, writing for *A Noite,* translating films, preparing radio programs, and writing occasional articles in English for the *New York Times, Theatre Arts,* and other periodicals.

In 1950 he was elected a Rio de Janeiro councilman, a post that he held, through reelection, until 1958. In 1959 he was appointed director of the Department of History and Documentation of the state of Guanabara.

"The Immunizer" ("Corpo Fechado") is from *Fuga e Outros Contos,* 1936.

Mário de Andrade

It Can Hurt Plenty

You remember Teresinha whose husband went to jail for killing those two brothers, Aldo and Tino? In an indirect sort of way it was Teresinha who really killed them. And she suffered plenty, what with her two kids and no husband. But anyway, his sacrifice seemed to break the hex she put on people. Nobody committed any more crimes on account of her. Only, poor Alfredo was stuck in that retreat up the river, slowly chewing and swallowing the twenty years that his nemesis of a mate cooked up for him. Injustice, bitterness . . . things that are hard to digest. Result: Alfredo had such a stomachache that he became one of the most unwelcome guests in the penitentiary. Nobody liked him and he was always in some kind of trouble. I'm wasting too much time on him.

Teresinha suffered, poor thing! She was still half-goodlooking, with a nice shape. She could brag that lots of guys wanted to sleep with her and were even willing to pay for it. She refused. At first because she was thinking of Alfredo the beloved; then later because she was thinking of Alfredo the murderer. She was sometimes on the point of giving in, but then she pictured Alfredo coming out of the penitentiary with a new knife in his hand to disembowel her. So she stayed virtuous in a cold sweat. She got no pleasure out of life. She was angry at the whole situation and she didn't have any outlet, so she'd come home and take it out on whoever was weaker than she was. She'd see her mother, prematurely old and practically dying on her feet, take five minutes to lift a suit of long underwear out of the washtub. Right away she'd throw some more dirty wash at her.

"If you don't look out, you'll fall asleep with that stuff in your hands."

She was home. But could you really call it a home? It looked like one of those road huts where the mule drivers rest. Just about as dirty. Two things that looked vaguely like chairs. One table. One bed. On the floor there was a mattress where the cockroaches lived. At night they came out and danced on the old lady's face. After all, where do all the insects of this world perform their tribal dances? On somebody's face, right?

There was another room, where nobody slept. Small and stuffy. A tiny stove was there, but sometimes for two days in a row nobody lit a match because that would have implied food to cook and coal to burn, of each of which there was often none. But the stove was there, so in Teresinha's and her mother's dictionary it had the grand name of kitchen.

They lived in this hut with Teresinha's whelp, who was a sort of leftover—in every sense of the term. How could Teresinha spare any feeling for him? Good heavens, living with all kinds of injustice, wanting a man and not having any, thinking all the time about what Alfredo might do to her, and with the death of the two brothers on her conscience. . . . And all she had in her hands, dipped in the gentle water, was somebody's underwear and socks, hardened with seven days' sweat. Some of her customers owed her for two weeks, and she hated them. . . . So, you see, Teresinha was carrying quite a burden. And as if this wasn't enough to plug up the fountain of maternal love, she had to put up with her pest of a mother-in-law, a big mulatto woman, whom she despised but needed because of the ten milreis she left there every month. The *figlia dun cane* would strut up to the house, very superior because she had maybe thirty contos in the bank, and would find fault with everything.

How could Teresinha feel any love for the little guy? She was a grown woman who never had any real fun in her entire thirty years on earth. She had a warm, live body and a cold, dead soul. . . . Paulino was almost four, and not since the first eight months did he know what it was to feel the warmth of her breast with her arms hugging him and her mouth coming close to his face and saying *figlioulo mio* and then giving him a noisy little sucking kiss, a mother's kiss . . .

Paulino was just a leftover in that house. And he was all the more so because his smart older brother, when he saw that everything was going to pot, had his guardian angel put a typhoid microbe on his tongue. The microbe went down to his little belly and started having children of its own, millions every hour, and within two nights they had paraded around there so much that they wore out the pavement. And off went the unbaptized soul to the limbo of innocent pagans. Paulino was left over.

Being a logical little fellow he never thought he was a leftover, because in that house he never saw anything left over. Paulino grew up on hunger, hunger was his daily bread. Sometimes, in the small hours of the night, he would wake up terrified. His angel was standing there. His guardian angel? Hell, no. His wicked angel, waking him up so he wouldn't die. The miserable kid would open his eyes in the foul-smelling dark and would half understand that he was eating himself up inside. The first few times he wept.

"Stá zito guaglion!"

What do you mean, *stá zito!* Did you ever feel real hunger gnawing at your entrails? . . . Paulino would sometimes stand up on his bowlegs and, with a sort of rocking gait, go over to his mother's bed. Bed, did I say? She hurt her foot and didn't have any money for the doctor who fixed it up. She had a choice: she could either get into the bed with the doctor or sell it to pay him. She sold it. Then she cut the mattress in two and put one half on top of three big boxes. That was the bed.

Teresinha woke up out of a sound sleep with her son's little hand patting her face. In a rage she struck out blindly, hitting him in the eyes and then in the pit of the stomach, wham! Paulino rolled on the floor. He wanted to scream, but his body reminded him of once when he cried too loud and got hit in the mouth with the heel of his mother's wooden slipper, and so he lost his taste for screaming. He just whimpered, so softly that it sort of lulled Teresinha back to sleep. He was all curled up very small like a pill bug. His pain and anguish were so intense that he paid no attention to the pinching of hunger. Finally he fell asleep.

In the cold early dawn his body woke up, and Paulino was surprised to find himself sleeping on the floor, far away from his grandmother's mattress. He had an ache in his shoulder, another in his knee, another in the part of his forehead that had been against the floor. But he hardly noticed these aches because of the immense pain of the cold. He crawled apprehensively, for the beginning of day outside was throwing ghostly glimmers through the cracks in the wall. He scared away the cockroaches and curled in the illusory warmth of his grandmother's bones. He didn't fall asleep again.

Finally, about six o'clock, Paulino was brought back to a consciousness of life in the world by the sound of the first people in the street: milkmen, baker's men, and food venders of all sorts. His body felt a vague warmth. The noises outside woke Teresinha. She stretched and sat up, vibrating with that matutinal sensuality that drives a person crazy with longing. She pressed her arms against her well-developed breasts and against her belly and all, and pressed her thighs together so hard it hurt around the kidneys. That restless, aimless hatred started up again. It came from a chastity preserved at great cost, a chastity which she herself knew must end sooner or later. She looked for her wooden slipper. Then she screamed at her mother: what was she doing in bed at this hour, why hadn't she put water in the tub, etcetera.

Before the women got up, Paulino had left the warmth of his place on the mattress and was prowling about the kitchen, for the grandest thing that ever happened to him was imminent: he was going to get something to eat, a piece of bread. It was a glorious holiday for him when a customer paid, or his rich grandmother came, or anything like that, because then, in addition to the bread, they had coffee with sugar! He always drank it too fast, that hot water flavored with a pinch of coffee, burning his tongue and his pale little lips. And then he went and ate his bread outside the house.

Not right in front of the house, for that's where the faucet, the tubs, and the bleaching stone were. The two women would be doing the washing there and fighting. Before long, they'd turn their wrath on him and, as a bonus, they'd give him a knuckle rap on the top of his head. Don't kid yourself, a knuckle rap can hurt; it can hurt plenty.

So he never ate there any more. He'd open the kitchen door— it never closed all the way—and go down the step. Then he'd run off, laughing for joy at his companion, the cold, and lose himself in the tall grass and the cocklebur thickets behind the house. This was his forest. Here Paulino nursed his sorrows without anyone seeing or scolding. He sat on the ground or stood with his heel on an ant heap, and began to eat. Then all of a sudden, ouch! He almost fell as he raised his little leg to kill the sauba ant that had its stingers embedded in his ankle. He picked up his bread, now buttered with dirt, and went on with his breakfast, enjoying the music of the grit as it crunched between his teeth. It sounded like a maraca.

But he didn't forget about the ant. When he had finished his bread, the boy warrior in him took over and he didn't even notice that he was still hungry. He looked for a piece of wood suitable for the hunting of ants in the great forest—a stunted forest, alas, penetrated by even the weakest sun.

With stick in hand he set out in search of ants. Not ordinary little ants; he couldn't be bothered with them. Only sauba ants. When he found one, he followed it patiently, breaking through the branches of the shrubs when necessary. Often his hand or leg burned because he had brushed against the stinging hairs of a butterfly larva. When he finally got the sauba ant into the open, he spent hours playing with the little wretch, until it died.

Then he felt hungry again. The sun was high, but Paulino knew that only after the factory whistles blew would there be beans and rice when things were going well or another piece of bread when they weren't. He tried to distract himself by hunting for another sauba ant, but it didn't work. His daily suffering from hunger induced a mood of meditative melancholy. He would sit down, turn his head, and rest his cheek on his hand. Then one day, in the lacy shade of a bush, he learned how to forget his hunger for a while by falling asleep. He never dreamed in his sleep. The flies came and buzzed around his open mouth, attracted by the vestige of sweetness. Paulino stirred a little, pressed his tormented lips together, spread his legs a bit, and urinated.

Paulino woke up long before the time for the factories to whistle. He passed his tongue over his lips and chewed. There was the grit with its rhythmic scrunch—and something more, something small and sweetish, in his mouth. He took it out with his fingers to see what it was. It was two flies. Yes, flies. Didn't you know they tasted sort of sweet? He put them on his tongue, sucked their flavor, and swallowed them.

This was the beginning of a sustained effort to hide his hunger from himself by eating everything in the forest that could possibly be swallowed. Instead of wasting time hunting for sauba ants, he treated himself to little picnics of damp earth. Then he found something better. With tongue in readiness he would place his cheek on the ground next to an anthill. When an ant appeared he would shoot out his tongue, which soon became skilled in this maneuver. He would retract his tongue with the ant stuck to it and would press the infinitesimally small, round thing against the roof of his mouth. He'd place it between his teeth, crush it, and swallow his saliva—an illusion of eating. And what a bonanza if he came upon a whole line of ants! He'd get on his knees, with his backside to the clouds, and lick the ground like an anteater. In twenty seconds he could liquidate a procession a yard long.

Once, in this effort to kill his hunger, Paulino descended from the high epicurean level that I've been describing: he caught a cockroach, put it in his mouth, and chewed it as he walked away. Totally unaware that he was doing something disgusting. Of course, you must bear in mind that these things he ate provided almost no nourishment. The factory would whistle, and the prospect of rice and beans found Paulino sated, his belly filled with illusions. He grew weaker and weaker. He looked as bleak as a day in midwinter.

Teresinha never noticed. The rein of virtue was by then so spent that the mare would soon break free and run wild. As a warm-up, she clouted Paulino—blindly, at random, her blows landing on every part of his body.

Fernandez the carter generally walked her home these days. He was an erect young fellow, of decent family, no more than twenty-five years old, and somewhat slow in his mental processes but physically energetic. The rein broke. Teresinha let him carry her bundle of wash, he came into the house, and she offered him coffee and consent. The old lady dirtied her mouth with some filthy language that no one exactly understood, took her mattress and her utterly astounded grandson, and moved into the kitchen.

Anyway, the meals improved and the little belly learned the secret delights of baked macaroni. Only, he was afraid of the

man. Fernandez had made a little fuss over him when he first
came into the house. The next morning, when they were all having breakfast together, Paulino began to play with one of the
man's long legs and got a shove that left him with his ears
drooping.

Naturally, the mother-in-law learned what was going on and
came over. Teresinha was embarrassed. She said good-morning
and got barked at in reply. But Teresinha didn't need the mulatto
woman's money any more and so she came back at her like a
wildcat. A terrifying scene! Paulino wanted to run away, but he
stood there fascinated because the mother-in-law kept pointing
to him and saying "my grandson" every other second. She said
Teresinha would have to get along without her help now, because
she wasn't going to pay for any hanky-panky of a cheap Italian
girl with a Spaniard. Teresinha shouted that a Spaniard was a
lot better than a Brazilian any day, you daughter of a Negro!
Mother of a murderer! I don't need you, you understand? Mulatto! Mother of a murderer!

"You're the murderer, you pig! You made my son do it, you
damned wop, you pig!"

"Get out of here, mother of a murderer! You never bothered
with your grandson before, and now all of a sudden you're worried about him. Take him along with you if you want to."

"I'll take him all right! Poor innocent little thing, he doesn't
know what kind of a mother he has. You pig! Pig!"

She picked up Paulino with one arm and, adjusting her Sunday
shawl, walked quickly away. A few women of the neighborhood
looked with curiosity at her and the boy, who was kicking furiously. To show these onlookers that she was in the right, she
turned around and shouted:

"Listen! I'm not going to pay your rent any more. I protected you because you were the wife of my unfortunate son,
but I'm not going to support a loose woman, understand?"

Teresinha, mad with hate, was already looking around for a
piece of wood with which to beat her mother-in-law to death.
The older woman thought it prudent to quit while she was ahead
and stalked off in triumph, clump, clump.

Paulino, jostled rhythmically against all that warm flesh, wept
with fear. He was bewildered: a street he had never seen before,

lots of people, this strange-acting woman, and he without mother, without bread, without his forest, without grandma. . . . What was happening to him? Terror crept through his little bluish body, but he was afraid to cry very loudly because he noticed that the old lady was wearing shoes with big heels, bigger even than the heels on wooden slippers. If she ever hit him in the mouth with one of those heels, it would tear his lips to pieces. . . . And Paulino, horror-stricken, forced his hands into his mouth, thus inventing a kind of mute.

"My poor grandson!"

With her big, warm hand she took his little head and placed it against her rubbery neck. It was sort of nice being carried in those strong arms, with the shawl providing extra warmth. . . . And the old woman looking at him with eyes of compassion and comfort. . . . My heavens, what is all this, that makes a fellow feel so good? Don't you know, Paulino? It's affection, that's what it is. It's tenderness. It's love. The old lady hugged him against her breast, placed his cheek against hers, and then kissed him again and again. In short, she introduced the kid to the great mystery.

Paulino became calmer. For the first time in his life, his concept of the future extended all the way to the next day. He felt he was protected and that tomorrow he would certainly have coffee and sugar. For hadn't the old woman put her mouth to his face and given him those big, wonderfully noisy kisses? And so Paulino's thoughts extended to tomorrow, and he imagined a huge cup, as big as the old lady, filled to the brim with coffee and sugar. He smiled at the two tears running down her cheeks, but then he saw, in the middle of one of the tears, a shoe . . . growing, growing, until its heel was as big as the old lady. Paulino began to cry softly again, as he did back home in the early morning when his crying served Teresinha as a lullaby. Until she woke up and screamed at him:

"For Christ's sake, that's enough! Get up now. Come on!"

The heel grew longer, enormously longer, and became the chimney of a building on the other side of the street. Paulino, choked with fear, stopped sobbing. They had arrived.

This was a real house. You went in by the garden, with flowers, and you wanted to pick all the roses. You went up a few

stairs and there was a parlor with two big pictures on the wall—
a man and a woman. The woman was the old lady. Plenty of
chairs, and one big one on which lots of people could sit at the
same time. On a small table in the middle of the room, there
was a vase with a pink flower that never withered. And those
little white doilies on the chairs and on the table, they could
keep you amused just counting the round tassels. The rest of the
house was just as amazing.

Afterwards, two very pretty girls appeared, wearing the navy-
blue skirts and white blouses of normal-school students. They
stared unpleasantly at him. Those four dark eyes came down
like hard knuckles on the skull of Paulino's soul. He stood glued
to the floor, motionless, dizzy.

Then there was a terrible row. The old lady made some re-
mark and one of the girls replied crossly. The old lady raised
her voice and spoke of "my grandson." The other girl shouted
at her, and there came a tempest of "my grandson" and "your
grandson," with lightning striking all around Paulino's head. It
got worse and worse. When the three voices could rise no higher,
the old lady slapped the girl nearer her and aimed a spoon at
the head of the other one, but she ducked and ran out of the
room.

Paulino's imagination couldn't have conjured up a more terrifying situation. And the funny thing is that, for the first time,
terror awakened his intelligence. His prior concept of the next
day disappeared, and Paulino saw that there would be nothing
but anger and abuse tomorrow and tomorrow and more than
three million years of tomorrows.

"Go pick up that spoon!"

His bowlegs moved, God knows how. He picked up the spoon
and gave it to the old lady. She put it away and left the dining
room. Everything was settled, the room was empty. The shadows
of late afternoon came in quickly and hid the unknown objects.
Only the table stood out clearly, especially the red and white
stripes of the tablecloth. Paulino leaned against one of the table
legs. He was trembling. A nice sizzling sound and a delicious
smell came from inside, and a soothing ticktock seemed to be
trying to calm him.

Paulino sat on the floor. A great peace settled on his exhausted mind: he had nothing to fear from the old lady's heel. She wasn't like his mother. When she got angry she didn't throw a shoe, she just threw a light little spoon, all gleaming and silver. Paulino curled up, his cheek against the floor. He was so sleepy after all he had been through. There was no more danger of a rap in the teeth with the heel of a wooden slipper; the old mulatto woman would only throw a silver spoon at him. And Paulino didn't know whether a silver spoon could hurt. He fell asleep.

"Get up off the floor! How this child must have suffered, Margot! See how skinny he is."

"No wonder! With his mother enjoying herself in orgies day and night, what would you expect!"

"Margot . . . you know what 'whore' means, don't you? Well, I think Paulino is what the old writers used to call a whoreson."

They laughed.

"Margot!"

"Yes?"

"Send Paulino here so he can get something to eat."

"Go in there, boy."

The bandy legs rocked rapidly as Paulino went into the kitchen. He soon learned that in this room he must not move around or touch anything. The kind old lady pushed the door mat with her foot.

"Sit down there and eat everything, you hear?"

It was rice and beans. With longing eyes he watched the meat disappear through the door to the dining room. The old lady probably thought that a boy of four didn't need meat, especially in view of the financial burden of bringing up two daughters.

Paulino's life was still miserable, but the nature of the misery had changed. The food had improved and there was enough of it, yet Paulino was haunted by a longing for the things he used to eat in his little forest. The old mulatto woman never suffered any recurrence of tenderness. It must have been a sort of reflex associated with a sense of duty. Those kisses she gave him were sincere all right, but only within the framework of tragedy. When the tragedy, as she saw it, was ended, so was the tenderness. She left Paulino with a terrible yearning for kisses.

He wanted to be close to the two girls, but they were always annoyed with him and pinched him for no apparent reason. Nevertheless, the younger, Nininha, who had an immense curiosity and who never got grades as high as Margot's, took it upon herself to give Paulino his bath. When Saturday came, she put him in the tub. He was amazed. He was also scared that he'd get pinched again. But instead he felt the caress of a face, hot and pretty, rubbing against his little body. The bath always ended with her angry at him and putting the nightshirt on him very fast, almost brutally. "Stand up straight, you pest!" she'd say, and she'd give him a twisting sort of pinch. It hurt, it hurt.

Paulino went down the kitchen steps and walked listlessly along the alleyway at the side of the house leading to the front garden. With considerable effort he pulled open the gate, which was always slightly ajar. He went out, sat down, rested his cheek on his hand with his head turned sideways, and watched the world go by.

And so, between pinches and hard words, most of which he did not understand, he too went by, like the world: sad, bewildered, afraid, tied to the earth, and progressively failing. But what could he do? He would drink his coffee and they would tell him to eat his bread in the yard or—pig!—he'd mess up the whole house. He went to the yard. The earth was so moist, it was a terrible temptation. Not that he thought of it as a temptation, for no one threatened him with a knuckle rap on the head if he ate earth. *Treck-trrleck,* he chewed a little piece, swallowed it, chewed another little piece, swallowed it. And then, around ten o'clock, he had to sit down on that doormat, with its fibers always pricking him, and had to swallow beans and rice, which he found nauseating.

"Good heavens, this boy doesn't eat! Just see how he looks at his food! Why do you get earth all over your face like a pig, eh?"

Paulino was afraid he'd get a rap with a spoon, and so he swallowed some beans, dry. Then the old lady's mind suddenly clicked.

"Is it possible! . . . You've been eating earth, haven't you? Let me see."

She pulled Paulino to the door of the kitchen and, with those two enormous, hot hands:

"Open your mouth, boy!"

She drew back his lips. Earth between his teeth and on his gums.

"Open your mouth, I told you!"

And her fingers opened his little mouth wide. She looked at his tongue. It was the color of earth all the way back to the root. Paulino got hit so often he thought it would never end. First came a slap on the mouth, which was still open, making a funny sort of sound, pah! Then came an avalanche of slaps, wallops, twisting pinches, knuckle raps on the head. And nasty words, which for little kids are also slaps in the face, right?

Then began Paulino's greatest martyrdom. Nobody wanted him to be in the house, he practically had to live in the backyard. Along with his bread he always got a tongue lashing of threats that almost knocked him out, honest to God! Paulino went down the steps to the yard, munching his bread. He was dazed. He felt the whole world hitting him. And then? . . . The bread was gone, and the tasty earth was still there, calling to him, offering itself to him. But those three women, those pinchers, didn't want him to eat it. . . . Oh, what a temptation to our poor little Saint Anthony! He wanted to eat it but he couldn't. Well, he could, but then the old lady would come and stick her big fingers in his mouth. . . . To eat or not to eat? . . . He fled his temptation, climbed the steps, and sat down, looking at the wall of the house so that he could not see the good earth. But it was there, calling him, all his, just five small steps below . . .

Luckily, he suffered this temptation only three days, for then he started to cough. It got worse and worse. The old lady was fit to be tied. Paulino heard her say it was one of those rasping coughs that are so annoying. Maybe he caught it from the boys across the street; he was playing with them in front of the gate. Let's give him the syrup that Dona Emilia taught us how to make. But Dona Emilia's syrup didn't help, nor did the five milreis spent for a patent medicine at the cut-rate drugstore. He just had to wait and hope that the cough would lose its voice and slink away by itself.

Paulino didn't like the scratchy feeling in his throat. He swallowed a lot to see if he could make it stop. When he got a coughing attack he went over to a wall and leaned against it.

His eyes were running, his nose was running, and he was dribbling from the mouth, which he kept open all the time. The little guy sat down wherever he was, because otherwise he would have fallen. The chair was spinning, the table was spinning, even the smell in the kitchen was spinning. Paulino felt nauseous and his whole body hurt.

"Poor thing! Look, go cough outside, you're getting the floor all dirty. Go on!"

Fear gave Paulino the necessary strength, and he went out. He had another attack. He lay down, his mouth pressed against the earth, but with no desire to eat. For a long time he was stretched out on the ground without moving. His body didn't hurt any more. His head didn't think any more. He just stayed there. The dampness of the ground would have made his cough worse and he might have died, but he finally got up. He wanted to go back into the house. But he might get it dirty and then they'd pinch him in the chest. And it wouldn't do any good anyway, because they'd just send him right out again. . . .

It was late afternoon. Street cars were going by, carrying the workers home. Paulino sat down at the front gate and watched them with his moist eyes. Night would fall soon, bringing new life. A light, dusty April wind touched his cheek. The sun, clutching in vain at the horizon, stained the tired air of day with red and green. The groups of workers walking past looked almost black against the sky. Everything was mysterious in contrasted light and shadow.

At that moment Teresinha came walking down the street. Stunningly dressed. To start from the bottom: her shoes were a dull yellow, her stockings gave a pink glow to her pretty legs, which were revealed up to the knee, and her dress was of a light blue lovelier than the April sky. And mama's face, how beautiful it was, with some of that dark hair done up in a lustrous topknot and some of it drawn from the center across her forehead, giving a glow of Neapolitan blue to the swarthy skin, which was illuminated also by the colors of French cosmetics.

With a confusion of joyous instincts in his body, and not exactly aware of what he was doing, Paulino got up.

"Mama!"

Teresinha turned. It was her *figlioulo*. I don't know just what happened in her mind, but she ran to him and kneeled down on the sidewalk in her silk stockings. She hugged Paulino against her ample breasts. It hurt, but deliciously. And Teresinha cried, because after all she was very unhappy too. Fernandez had walked out on her and, after some indecision, she had become a full-time prostitute. Now, seeing Paulino so dirty and sick-look-ing, she suddenly had an impulse to give up the life she was living. She cried in remorse and self-pity.

Only then did she feel badly about her son, so horribly thin and more fragile than virtue. He must have been suffering there in the mulatto woman's house. . . . For a moment she considered taking Paulino with her. But she quickly hid the thought from herself, for he would obviously be in the way whenever . . . She looked at his clothes. They weren't of the very best material, but they were serviceable. She placated her conscience by pretending to think that her son was being treated well. She planted a kiss on the little mouth, moist with phlegm, and swallowed a tear. Then she hugged him and kissed him several times. She walked off, adjusting her clothes.

Paulino, not very firm on his feet, made no motion, no ges-ture. He watched the blue dress disappear in the distance. He turned away. A piece of greasy wrapping paper was rolling merrily on the ground. He would have to take three steps to catch it. . . . It wasn't worth it. He sat on the step again. The colors of the evening were gently blending into a common gray. Paulino rested his cheek on the palm of his hand. In an indiffer-ence born of exhaustion, he half heard, half saw the world about him. His mouth was open; phlegm and saliva ran out onto his hand. From there it dripped on his shirt, which was dark so that it wouldn't show the dirt.

*   *   *

Mário de Andrade (1893–1945), a native of São Paulo, where he spent most of his life, has been called the vastest and most cul-tured mind in Brazilian modernism, as well as its great *animador* (encourager, stimulator). A versatile, experimental, and prolific writer, he produced several volumes of poetry, three books of short stories, a novel, a number of books on music, and essays on art and literature, as well as voluminous correspondence, including lengthy letters to other writers, some of them young and obscure. He also did research in folklore, which he utilized in a curious volume of narrative described as a "rhapsody." Mário de Andrade said that he held forth his works not as solutions of any sort, not even possible or temporary solutions, but as "searchings." He believed that his fiction represented him more genuinely than his other writings did, but this opinion has been challenged.

Apart from his literary career, he worked at certain times as a music teacher, as a professor of aesthetics, and as a public servant. From 1934 to 1937 he directed the Culture Department of the City of São Paulo.

"It Can Hurt Plenty" ("Piá Não Sofre? Sofre") is from *Contos de Belazarte*, 1934.

Rachel de Queiroz

Metonymy, or the Husband's Revenge

Metonymy. I learned the word in 1930 and shall never forget it. I had just published my first novel. A literary critic had scolded me because my hero went out into the night "chest unclosed."

"What deplorable nonsense!" wrote this eminently sensible gentlemen. "Why does she not say what she means? Obviously, it was his shirt that was unclosed, not his chest."

I accepted the rebuke with humility, indeed with shame. But my illustrious Latin professor, Dr. Matos Peixoto, came to my rescue. He said that what I had written was perfectly correct; that I had used a respectable figure of speech known as metonymy; and that this figure consisted in the use of a word for another word associated with it—for example, a word representing a cause instead of the effect, or representing the container when the content is intended. The classic instance, he told me, is "the sparkling cup"; in reality, not the cup but the wine in it is sparkling.

The professor and I wrote a letter, which was published in the newspaper where the review had appeared. It put my unjust critic in his place. I hope he learned a lesson. I know I did. Ever since, I have been using metonymy—my only bond with classical rhetoric.

Moreover, I have devoted some thought to it, and I have concluded that metonymy may be more than a figure of speech. There is, I believe, such a thing as practical or applied metonymy. Let me give a crude example, drawn from my own experience. A certain lady of my acquaintance suddenly moved out of the boardinghouse where she had been living for years and became a mortal enemy of the woman who owned it. I asked her why. We both knew that the woman was a kindly soul; she had given my friend injections when she needed them, had often loaned her a hot-water bag, and had always waited on her when she had her little heart attacks. My friend replied:

"It's the telephone in the hall. I hate her for it. Half the time when I answered it, the call was a hoax or joke of some sort."

"But the owner of the boardinghouse didn't perpetrate these hoaxes. She wasn't responsible for them."

"No. But whose telephone was it?"

I know another case of applied metonymy, a more disastrous one for it involved a crime. It happened in a city of the interior, which I shall not name for fear that someone may recognize the parties and revive the scandal. I shall narrate the crime but conceal the criminal.

Well, in this city of the interior there lived a man. He was not old but he was spent, which is worse than being old. In his youth he had suffered from beriberi. His legs were weak, his chest was tired and asthmatic, his skin was yellowish, and his eyes were rheumy. He was, however, a man of property: he owned the house in which he lived and the one next to it, in which he had set up a grocery store. Therefore, although so unattractive personally, he was able to find himself a wife. In all justice to him, he did not tempt fate by marrying a beauty. Instead, he married a poor, emaciated girl, who worked in a men's clothing factory. By her face one would have thought she had consumption. So our friend felt safe. He did not foresee the effects of good nutrition and a healthful life on a woman's appearance. The girl no longer spent eight hours a day at a sewing table. She was the mistress of her house. She ate well: fresh meat, cucumber salad, pork fat with beans and manioc mush, all kinds of sweets, and oranges, which her husband bought by the gross for his customers. The effects were like magic. Her body filled out, especially in the best places. She even seemed to grow taller. And her face—what a change! I may have forgot to mention that her features, in themselves, were good to begin with. Moreover, money enabled her to embellish her natural advantages with art: she began to wear makeup, to wave her hair, and to dress well.

Lovely, attractive, she now found her sickly, prematurely old husband a burden and a bore. Each evening, as soon as the store was closed, he dined, mostly on milk (he could not stomach meat), took his newspaper, and rested on his chaise longue until time to go to bed. He did not care for the movies or for soccer or for radio. He did not even show much interest in love. Just a sort of tepid, tasteless cohabitation.

And then Fate intervened: it produced a sergeant.

Granted, it was unjust for a young wife, after being reconditioned at her husband's expense, to employ her charms to the prejudice of the aforesaid husband. Unjust; but, then, this world thrives on injustice, doesn't it? The sergeant—I shall not say whether he was in the Army, the Air Force, the Marines, or the Fusileers, for I still mean to conceal the identities of the parties— the sergeant was muscular, young, ingratiating, with a manly, commanding voice and a healthy spring in his walk. He looked gloriously martial in his high-buttoned uniform.

One day, when the lady was in charge of the counter (while her husband lunched), the sergeant came in. Exactly what happened and what did not happen, is hard to say. It seems that the sergeant asked for a pack of cigarettes. Then he wanted a little vermouth. Finally, he asked permission to listen to the sports broadcast on the radio next to the counter. Maybe it was just an excuse to remain there awhile. In any case, the girl said it would be all right. It is hard to refuse a favor to a sergeant, especially a sergeant like this one. It appears that the sergeant asked nothing more that day. At most, he and the girl exchanged expressive glances and a few agreeable words, murmured so softly that the customers, always alert for something to gossip about, could not hear them.

Three times more the husband lunched while his wife chatted with the sergeant in the store. The flirtation progressed. Then the husband fell ill with a grippe, and the two others went far beyond flirtation. How and when they met, no one was able to discover. The important thing is that they were lovers and that they loved with a forbidden love, like Tristan and Isolde or Paolo and Francesca.

Then Fate, which does not like illicit love and generally punishes those who engage in it, transferred the sergeant to another part of the country.

It is said that only those who love can really know the pain of separation. The girl cried so much that her eyes grew red and swollen. She lost her appetite. Beneath her rouge could be seen the consumptive complexion of earlier times. And these symptoms aroused her husband's suspicion, although, curiously, he had never suspected anything when the love affair was flourishing and everything was wine and roses.

He began to observe her carefully. He scrutinized her in her periods of silence. He listened to her sighs and to the things she murmured in her sleep. He snooped around and found a postcard and a book, both with a man's name in the same handwriting. He found the insignia of the sergeant's regiment and concluded that the object of his wife's murmurs, sighs, and silences was not only a man but a soldier. Finally he made the supreme discovery: that they had indeed betrayed him. For he discovered the love letters, bearing airmail stamps, a distant postmark, and the sergeant's name. They left no reasonable doubt.

For five months the poor fellow twisted the poisoned dagger of jealousy in his thin, sickly chest. Like a boy who discovers a birds' nest and, hiding nearby, watches the eggs increasing in number every day, so the husband, using a duplicate key to the wood chest where his wife put her valuables, watched the increase in the number of letters concealed there. He had given her the chest during their honeymoon, saying, "Keep your secrets here." And the ungrateful girl had obeyed him.

Every day at the fateful hour of lunch, she replaced her husband at the counter. But he was not interested in eating. He ran to her room, pulled out a drawer of her bureau, removed the chest from under a lot of panties, slips, and such, took the little key out of his pocket, opened the chest, and anxiously read the new letter. If there was no new letter, he reread the one dated August 21st; it was so full of realism that it sounded like dialogue from a French movie. Then he put everything away and hurried to the kitchen, when he swallowed a few spoonfuls of broth and gnawed at a piece of bread. It was almost impossible to swallow with the passion of those two thieves sticking in his throat.

When the poor man's heart had become utterly saturated with jealousy and hatred, he took a revolver and a box of bullets from the counter drawer; they had been left, years before, by a customer as security for a debt, which had never been paid. He loaded the revolver.

One bright morning at exactly ten o'clock, when the store was full of customers, he excused himself and went through the doorway that connected the store with his home. In a few seconds the customers heard the noise of a row, a woman's scream, and three shots. On the sidewalk in front of the shopkeeper's house they saw his wife on her knees, still screaming, and him, with the revolver in his trembling hand, trying to raise her. The front door of the house was open. Through it, they saw a man's legs, wearing khaki trousers and boots. He was lying face down, with his head and torso in the parlor, not visible from the street.

The husband was the first to speak. Raising his eyes from his wife, he looked at the terror-stricken people and spotted among them his favorite customer. He took a few steps, stood in the doorway, and said:

"You may call the police."

At the police station he explained that he was a deceived husband. The police chief remarked:

"Isn't this a little unusual? Ordinarily you kill your wives. They're weaker than their lovers."

The man was deeply offended.

"No," he protested, "I would be utterly incapable of killing my wife. She is all that I have in the world. She is refined, pretty, and hard-working. She helps me in the store, she understands bookkeeping, she writes the letters to the wholesalers. She is the only person who knows how to prepare my food; I have a special diet. Why should I want to kill my wife?"

"I see," said the chief of police. "So you killed her lover."

The man shook his head.

"Wrong again. The sergeant—her lover—was transferred to a place far away from here. I discovered the affair only after he had gone. By reading his letters. They tell the whole story. I know one of them by heart, the worst of them. . . ."

The police chief did not understand. He said nothing and waited for the husband to continue, which he presently did:

"Those letters! If they were alive I would kill them, one by one. They were shameful to read—almost like a book. I thought of taking an airplane trip. I thought of killing some other sergeant here, so that they would all learn a lesson not to fool around with another man's wife. But I was afraid of the rest of the regiment; you know how these military men stick together. Still, I had to do something. Otherwise I would have gone crazy. I couldn't get those letters out of my head. Even on days when none arrived I felt terrible, worse than my wife. I had to put an end to it, didn't I? So today, at last, I did it. I waited till the regular time and, when I saw the wretch appear on the other side of the street, I went into the house, hid behind a door, and lay there for him."

"The lover?" asked the police chief stupidly.

"No, of course not. I told you that I didn't kill her lover. It was those letters. The sergeant sent them—but *he* delivered them. Almost every day, there he was at the door, smiling, with the vile envelope in his hand. I pointed the revolver and fired three times. He didn't say a word; he just fell. No, chief, it wasn't her lover. It was the mailman."

✳   ✳   ✳

Rachel de Queiroz was born in 1910 in Fortaleza, the capital of Ceará, but spent part of her childhood on a ranch in the backlands. In 1921 she was sent to live and study at a nun's school (in Fortaleza), which she fictionalized in one of her novels, published in English translation as *The Three Marias*. At the age of nineteen, when she was a teacher at a normal school in Fortaleza, she produced a successful novel about a drought in the northeast. In addition to novels, Rachel de Queiroz has written plays and newspaper columns. For the past twenty years she has contributed a column to the popular weekly magazine *O Cruzeiro*. She is admired for, among other things, her simplicity of style and her liveliness of both style and thought.

In 1931 she joined the Communist Party, from which she was expelled in 1933 as a Trotzkyite; she describes her present position, which she has held for many years, as moderate socialism. She is married to a physician and lives in Rio de Janeiro. In 1966 she served as a Brazilian representative in the United Nations General Assembly.

"Metonymy, or the Husband's Revenge" ("Metonímia, ou a Vingança do Enganado") is from *Cem Crônicas Selecionadas*, 1958.

Marques Rebêlo

The Beautiful Rabbits

"They're real Angoras," said Manuel, the caretaker, eager to
have me appreciate his gift.

It was a warm November evening. At Aunt Bizuca's country
place, where I lived, the sapodilla trees in the orchard were beginning to bear their rich fruit.

Manuel had brought the two rabbits in a lidded basket. Now
he lifted them by their ears to exhibit them to me. I protested
this apparent barbarity, but he explained that it was the customary and correct way to lift rabbits.

Real Angoras or not, they were most dearly beloved. Pure
white except for their pink ears. Beautiful, adorable.

Until then my life had been a succession of toys and more
toys, of hide-and-seek and blindman's buff, of noise and harmless
mischief outdoors and in. So far as I knew, these were indeed
the sole purposes of childhood. It was Manuel's gift, those two
oh-so-white pompons, that made me see, beyond the carefree
world of fun, another and greater world, the world of obligations.
School reveals this world to most children, but my school was
very progressive and easy; the formal classes were few and I
could attend them or not, as I pleased. Moreover, Auntie had
told them not to push me ahead too fast.

So, as I said, the rabbits gave me my first real idea of duty.
Far from rebelling, however, I dedicated myself to my obligations
with infinite love and joy. "It's time to give the rabbits their
water"—and neither fire nor earthquake could have kept me
from the prompt performance of this task. I combed them, I
hunted for lice in their fur, I took them for walks in the rose
garden that Auntie loved so dearly. I even declined Taninho's
invitations to join him on the Sunday rides in his father's Benz.
I spent virtually all my time with them, the ever mobile inspira-

tions and objects of my meticulous care. I became the slave of these tiny, innocent tyrants.

I'll go farther and maintain that they were, in a measure, intelligent, responsive tyrants. What thoughts and sentiments lay hidden behind that bland whiteness! And so they initiated me not only into the world of obligations but also into the world of mutual affection.

I loved them with the tenderness of a sweetheart. I overwhelmed them with caresses. I hugged them so often and so hard that Auntie protested:

"Some day you're going to kill those animals, squeezing them like that."

I covered them with kisses. Forgetful of the clock, I spent hours in the remote corners of the house conversing with them, replying to their questions. I lost touch with reality, I failed to distinguish them one from the other, I blended them into one huge rabbit, bigger than any rabbit ever seen, almost as big as I, acting like a person, talking and laughing like a person, and dressed in a sailor suit like mine.

Along with love came love's usual cortege of woes. How many hours of torture you caused me, my adorable little beasts! I loved you too much not to suffer. Jealousy made its debut in my heart and, cannibalistic savage that it is, fairly devoured me. Nor was my jealousy unfounded, for I had a rival. And what a powerful, fierce rival, o angels of heaven! Silvino, a little colored houseboy two years older than I. His mother, a faithful servant who had given Aunt Bizuca her youth and had asked little in return, died in childbirth, and Auntie reared the boy.

Accordingly, if I enjoyed within the household the advantage of consanguinity, he enjoyed the prestige of seniority, and he used it with great success, especially among the servants. How often one of them would say to me:

"You wouldn't remember. It happened before you came here."

But Silvino remembered. Looking at me sideways with a barely perceptible, mocking smile, he would relate the thing in full, indeed superfluous, detail, for he knew that I would feel humiliated. He was the veteran, the old-timer; no one could deny it. And how you used this advantage, o cunning, all-too-human Silvino, to defend yourself from me, the intruder!

A terrible rival, astute and always ready to seize an opportunity. As I remember him, he had lively, meddlesome eyes, short, woolly hair, beautiful, strong, white teeth, and a round, monkeylike face which he could contort expertly into mischievous grimaces.

The caretaker's gift to me hurt Silvino. Why hadn't it been given to him? What had I done to deserve it? He had a better right to it than I. He helped Manuel take care of the place. He moved fertilizer in the wheelbarrow, he swept out the begonia hothouse, he brought Manuel his meals, he watered the plants for him, he helped him with the pruning of the fig trees that formed a compact green barrier protecting the property from the prying eyes of neighbors. It was only fair for him to get the present. But I had got it instead. Manuel was a great fool, a miserable bootlicker. And all because I was a nephew, that was the only reason.

Well, he hadn't got the present. So what? It didn't matter; he would fight on another front. He would win the affection of my bunnies. He would and he did. If, for example, I gave them some lettuce, he would replace it with better, for the vegetable garden withheld no secrets from him and he knew exactly where to find the lettuce with the freshest leaves and the tenderest hearts.

It was war, and I fought back with all my resources. After all, the rabbits were mine, weren't they? So get away, you thicklipped Negro! I carried them in my arms wherever I went, day and night. I didn't let him touch them, not even with one finger.

"You can look at them, that's all."

I would stroke them in front of him. He must have suffered intensely, but he never showed it. He just smiled and said to himself:

"My day will come."

It did come, the black day on which I had to change schools. The new one was businesslike and severe, with a definite daily schedule that I could not escape. For, as Aunt Bizuca said, I was a big boy now, I had to devote myself heart and soul to my studies so that I could be someone in the world. How dreadfully I suffered, only God knows. Interminable were the classes of Mr. Silva, who taught every subject, even physical exercise. Bored and boring, he was forever explaining to us in one lesson what we were going to take up in the next. Grammar, geography—

how could I care about verbs and nouns, how could it matter to me whether the world was round or flat, when my world was my rabbits!

Mr. Silva talked loudly but I hardly heard him. My thoughts were immersed in a cruel uncertainty: what was Silvino doing with my rabbits? My impatient eyes devoured the implacable clock in the hall, the infinitely long, echoing hall, with its ten windows looking out on the recreation yard. It was a sort of track on which the monitors ran noiselessly, surging up suddenly at the classroom door and surprising the incautious. What was Silvino doing? The hands of the clock never seemed to move. I lost my way in a labyrinth of conjectures: was he caressing them, scratching them, taking them out in the yard to feed?

"What have I just been talking about, Francisco?"

I didn't know. I was punished.

As soon as I got home I would throw my school bag in a corner, give Auntie a quick kiss, and run to see them. The whiteness of their fur revealed in no way the touch of the despised black hands. The pink eyes told me nothing. Mad with jealousy, I hit them. Their ears fell and they tried to run away. Then I would hug them, insanely, almost crying.

As we sat around after dinner, Auntie knitting, I doing my homework, the bandit would bring up the subject, just to hurt me:

"You know what, Francisco? Today I took your rabbits all the way to the baker's."

"Did you?"

Silvino could see that the wound was open and bleeding. He delighted in my agony.

"Well, I guess I'll go down and see if they're all right." And he would slowly leave the room, his hands in his pockets and a hard smile of vengeance at the corner of his mouth.

I could barely contain my rage; a little more and I would have burst. My penmanship at such moments deteriorated markedly. So did my arithmetic: I had twelve oranges left after starting with thirty-nine and giving fifteen to John.

May, gentle, placid May, brought to Auntie's house the molt of the canaries, some early tangerines, and Silvino's death. He had gone to the square to mail a letter and was run over by the ice truck.

He did not die immediately. He was carried home, screaming horribly. The clerk of the store led the way, waving people aside and excitedly explaining what had happened.

That night Silvino became delirious, and in his delirium he told of many little misdeeds he had committed. He had stolen bricks of guava paste from the pantry and spools of thread from the sewing basket. He had buried some demitasse spoons in the backyard. Most important, he cleared up the great mystery of the roses. Every morning for several months the ground of the rose garden had been found strewn with petals, even after a windless night. The high walls that surrounded the garden made this daily phenomenon all the more inexplicable. Aunt Bizuca, greatly concerned, finally accepted the solution suggested by Mrs. Silveira, a spiritist, that it was the work of some playful ghost who wanted to mystify people. But it was Silvino, possessed by heaven-knows-what voluptuousity. He had come at dawn each day (for he woke with the chickens) and had secretly torn off the petals.

Auntie laughed when Silvino revealed this unexpected explanation.

"So, you wily pickaninny, it was you, eh? Well, you just wait, you rascal."

She did not yet understand the seriousness of his injuries. The next morning Dr. Gouveia found that the X rays confirmed his diagnosis. He shook his head.

"Nothing more can be done for him," he told her. "He has a fracture of the pelvis and his spine is seriously affected. Only a miracle . . ." Dr. Gouveia always spoke precisely, laconically, scientifically.

"But, doctor . . ."

He interrupted her:

"I'll give him some morphine so he won't suffer so much."

From that moment on, Auntie devoted herself entirely to the patient. Tireless, tenderly affectionate, she was busy all day attending to one thing or another for him. She sat awake in his room four nights in succession. She had covered the bed lamp with brown paper, for the bright light bothered him.

On the fifth night at about eleven o'clock, Silvino stirred from the heavy torpor caused by the latest injection.

"Godmother," he murmured.

"What is it? I'm right here." And Auntie quickly emerged from the shadow, where she had been sitting on a stool, watching him.

"I know. Give me your hand."

She did, and he raised it, with difficulty, to his lips. Tears streamed from his eyes—those eyes, usually so round and alert, now dim and staring.

"Please, your blessing."

Auntie understood.

"What nonsense, my son! Sleep."

Son? Silvino, with a great effort, turned toward the lips that had spoken the word.

"Blessing, please. I don't want that pain anymore, God-mother."

He held her hand tightly, then suddenly released it. His head fell to the side by the wall.

"Good God! Francisco, Alexandrina! Bring a candle."

Everyone ran to the bedside. Auntie was already on her knees. We all kneeled and prayed. Someone lit a candle; it burned with a white light, very white, flickering yet brilliant, in the dark hand of the little corpse. Auntie sobbed.

Aunt Bizuca gave him a fine funeral. She had deep purple rings under her eyes. In her ample black dress, she seemed thin-ner, older.

"Poor Silvino!" she cried, in the consoling arms of the ladies of the neighborhood.

The house was full of people, for the little colored boy, impish but always ready to be helpful, had ingratiated himself with al-most everyone.

I was in the first taxi after the funeral coach. My face must have revealed my pleasure at the novel experience. Men on the street took off their hats as we passed. At the cemetery, in the warm, iridescent, smiling afternoon, I left Silvino forever. He was covered with roses, all the roses that Auntie's precious rose garden could supply. White roses, sisters of those which, for so long a time, he had despoiled.

Now I had the love of my rabbits all to myself. No longer need I listen to Silvino's long, loud, grating laugh. But my joy in the rabbits lasted only a short time. Perhaps the lack of competition removed a stimulus that had become essential. Or maybe my devotion to soccer, which began about that time, completely diverted my interest. In any event, the objects of my first love were abandoned. They lost their wonderful whiteness. Dirty, uncared for, they wandered forgotten through the yard and the gardens, wherever they wished, getting filthy in the mud, in the dust, or in the coal pile near the chicken coop.

When, from time to time, I met Manuel in the kitchen, he always said the same thing:

"Francisco is growing up. He doesn't think about rabbits anymore."

And, under his heavy eyebrows, he winked. In my confusion I would mutter some brief reply, hurry out into the hallway, and get far away from him as quickly as possible.

The lovely color of the rabbits' eyes faded. An opaque veil covered them and the rabbits soon became utterly blind. Their bellies were covered with swellings, which frightened Auntie.

"Mother of God! Do you think it can be bubonic plague?"

No, it was just old age, explained Manuel, who seemed to know everything about animals.

They died. Auntie, saddened, expected me to be sad too. I felt no grief at all, but I tried to conceal this evidence of miserable insensitivity.

"It's better this way, Auntie. The poor things were suffering so."

Auntie turned away.

"Yes, my son, you're right. It's better this way."

What I really felt was complete liberation. Soccer was my only interest. I played as a back. I played badly, like a child, but I played.

EDDY DIAS DA CRUZ, whose pseudonym is Marques Rebêlo, was born in 1907 in Rio de Janeiro, where he still resides. Like many other Brazilian intellectuals, he is a law graduate who never practiced law. He worked in commerce and, later, in industry but has discontinued these activities. Until recently, he served the federal government as a school inspector.

In the 1920's Marques Rebêlo contributed to modernist magazines and became a friend of Mário de Andrade and of Alcântara Machado. When, in the early 1930's, his books began to appear, the public was slow to recognize their merit, for at that time the violent novels of the northeast, wholly unlike Marques Rebêlo's work, were beginning their great vogue. In time, however, he achieved recognition as a master craftsman whose style, at once concise and lyrical, formed an ideal vehicle for his special combination of warmth and critical insight. In 1964 he was elected to the Brazilian Academy of Letters.

His works include short stories, novels, a play, newspaper columns, juvenile literature, accounts of travel, and an authoritative biography of the nineteenth-century author, Manuel Antônio de Almeida. He is now producing a seven-volume work of fiction, of which three volumes have already been published. He is represented in more than one hundred anthologies.

"The Beautiful Rabbits" ("Circo de Coelhinhos") is from *Três Caminhos,* 1933.

Graciliano Ramos

The Thief

The good luck that favored him during the first month or two turned out to be a misfortune. It was strange indeed: with no training at all this fellow starts out, makes one mistake after another, breaks into houses without studying the neighborhoods, clumps around as if he were out in the street—and everything goes fine. Clumping around like that, it's a miracle. You have to know how to move quickly and noiselessly, like a cat: your body must become weightless, it must float, almost leave the ground, and your legs must have spring and elasticity. Otherwise your joints will crack, you'll take forever to move from room to room, and the job will become almost impossible. But no one can achieve this necessary skill without an apprenticeship, and you can't complete an apprenticeship if you get caught at it.

Perhaps there is a divinity that protects novices, however brashly inept. At the beginning no one suspects them. They seem just like other people. The police don't follow them. If they didn't bump into furniture and shine their flashlights in the eyes of people who are sleeping, they'd probably never get arrested and sent to jail, which is a sort of trade school for thieves. That's where they sharpen their ears and get used to gliding around. After they're out they won't have to wear rope-soled shoes on the job any more: they'll move like machines with well-oiled springs, rolling silently on rubber tires.

The individual to whom I specifically refer had not yet acquired this indispensable if prejudicial manner: indispensable inside a house at night; prejudicial in the street, for it reveals the thief. Doubtless there are other signs by which a cop can recognize a thief, but the primary characteristic is this furtive, slinky way of walking, as if he were barely touching the ground. As I said, this fellow didn't know how to walk that way, and so he could pass unperceived in the crowd. There was no immediate likelihood that he could adopt the necessary, telltale manner. Sponger, his friend, who started him in the profession, had told him frankly that he ought to seek some less hazardous occupation. But the fellow was hard-headed. Encouraged by two or three lucky experiences, there he was, prowling around the iron gate as if he knew what he was doing.

He had already gained admission to the house by posing as a stove repairman and had observed the disposition of the furniture on the ground floor. He was sorry he hadn't studied the layout in greater detail. He should have got himself hired as a servant in the house for a week or so. That had been Sponger's advice, and Sponger could speak from experience. But, in his folly, he hadn't listened to him. So now he didn't even know on which side of the dining room the door to the pantry was located.

He moved away from the gate, afraid that someone might notice him. He walked down the street, entered a café at the corner, looked at the clock, and felt like taking a drink. He had no money. Besides, it would be crazy to drink at such a time. He was trembling. His hands were cold and damp.

"I've got to do it."

He looked again at the clock. It was after midnight. Fortunately, the street could be entered only at this end; at the other it came up against a hill. Few people, except those who lived on the street, were likely to go there.

... It really wasn't important. ... He worried for a moment about the possibility of running into someone who knew him. The trembling of his hands tormented him. He was almost certain the waiter had noticed how pale he was. He went outside and stood on the sidewalk, undecided, looking at the hill, wiping his damp fingers on his handkerchief, telling himself again that it wasn't important. He shook his head and tried to remember what wasn't important.

He felt like going home. But he smiled wryly and started up the street, staying always close to the walls of the houses. How could he go home? He lived in the streets. What wasn't important? Finally he remembered and he felt better. What wasn't important was whether the door to the pantry was on the left side or on the right side of the dining room. Should he go into the pantry and steal the silverware? Eh? No, it would increase the danger. But then he thought of the cheese he had seen on the refrigerator. His mouth watered.

As he approached the house, his legs felt weak. He was trembling like a child. Probably the pantry was on the right as you entered the dining room, near the stairway.

"I've got to do it."

He approached the house, circled the premises, and then stood with his back against the garden gate. If he stretched his neck to look down the street, the policeman (if there was one) on the corner might notice him. His heart beat desperately and his vision clouded. He could not even see the corner to determine whether a policeman was there.

He flattened his body still more closely against the gate. He looked at the window of the house on the opposite side of the street and imagined that someone was watching him from it, perhaps the owner of the dry-goods store who had stared ferociously at him through thick eyeglasses when he had approached the counter the day before. He tried to dismiss this troublesome thought. Why should he think that the same eyes which had immobilized him yesterday were looking at him now, especially at such an hour!

But suddenly panic seized him. He felt he was being observed from the front and the rear, so that he was impelled both to run away and to take refuge in the garden. The street was filled with ambushes. He began to tremble again. His thoughts became confused. It seemed to him, for a moment, that he had already finished the job. He leaned against the gate.

For several minutes he thought about his old school in the suburbs, and he saw himself as a sad, puny boy. The teacher seemed to ignore him. She rarely asked him questions. The evil-looking boy next to him used to stick him with a pin; when the boy grew up he became a soldier. The little girl with the braids was pretty; she had green eyes and whenever she spoke she shut them.

A shiver dispersed these memories. He wanted to smoke but was afraid to light a match. Raising his head, he was momentarily distracted by a trolley car far off at the end of the street.

... Yes, no, yes, no. ... His thoughts turned to the man behind the window, now comfortably warm and calm, and to the girl with the braids, smiling tranquilly and shutting her green eyes. His teeth chattered softly like castanets and then loudly like an angry pig. This alarmed him: perhaps someone could hear the noise. He bit into the sleeve of his jacket, stifling the sound.

Yes, no, yes, no. There was a clock in the dining room. He was almost sure he could hear the strokes of the pendulum. His teeth stopped chattering and further damage to his jacket was averted.

He stirred a little and stretched. His fears were subsiding. Now he moved with confidence. He grasped the top rail of the fence and, with a burst of energy, vaulted over into the garden. He crossed some flower beds and walked along the path to the porch. There he sank down on the sofa. If they found him so, he would say that he had entered the premises before the locking of the gate and had fallen asleep. That's what he'd say, although it would hardly serve to exculpate him.

But why dwell on possible misfortunes? He rose, went over to the door, and put his penknife in the lock. His hands no longer trembled. The bolt slid noiselessly. He stopped in surprise. He had never before worked alone, and he therefore expected every lock to stick. He had planned to climb up on the sofa and to cut, with a diamond, a piece of the glass panel above the door. He would then push an opened newspaper under the door, roll a handkerchief around his hand, and dislodge the glass, which would fall noiselessly on the paper. He would grasp the empty frame, pull himself up and, through the panel space, enter the house head first, groping for the floor. He would probably remain hanging there some time, like a monkey, with his curved toes serving as hooks on the lower edge of the opening. Almost surely something would go wrong in this maneuver. He would fail, he was bound to fail.

He looked for the glass panel. In vain: there was none. Nor did he have a newspaper. What stupidity to think this way, to invent trouble.

He opened the door and went in. He advanced slowly, afraid that he might bump into things. As his eyes became accustomed to the darkness, he began to distinguish vaguely the shapes of long, low chairs that cluttered the little parlor. He slid toward one of them and fell into it, exhausted, breathing fast, his heart pounding. The springs squeaked. He rose quickly and flattened himself against the wall. He was afraid his knees would give way. All the joints of his body seemed to crack whenever he moved; the noise would probably wake everybody up and he'd be captured. He lit his flashlight and was immediately sorry. What a rash thing to do! He turned it off.

He went into the dining room. Stretching his eyes wide he could see objects pretty clearly. A gray shadow extended down the stairway; there must have been a light on upstairs.

Fine: he could see the door to the pantry. It was on the right, just as he had thought. Two days before, he had seen a cheese on the refrigerator. He went over to the stairway and leaned on the banister with his head turned toward the pantry. He really wasn't hungry. He felt a pang in his stomach, but his mouth was dry. He shrugged his shoulders. It would be stupid to risk so much for a piece of cheese.

He went up one step and stopped. He was breathing hard. He climbed farther and felt nauseous. The stairway was moving, the house was moving. The dryness in his mouth disappeared. He puffed out his cheeks to contain the saliva as he thought about the cheese. He climbed a few more steps and swallowed the saliva with repugnance.

"I've got to do it."

He repeated this to strengthen his will. Yet, although he was halfway up the stairs, he found it difficult to continue. Suppose someone was watching him in the dark. He remembered the fellow in the dry-goods store; maybe he lived in this house and right now was staring at him like a cat. He thought again of the little girl in elementary school, of her smile, of her eyelids with which she hid her green eyes, like those of a cat. He hated himself for vacillating, for wasting time on such nonsense.

He arrived at the top of the stairs, stopped to listen, and then started down a hallway onto which many rooms opened. He went quickly past the door of a room where a light was on, and headed for the master bedroom, hoping it would not be in use. His fear was counterbalanced by a childish feeling of pride. He had done well so far. This job was quite an exploit, yes sir, and he wanted to hear what Sponger would say about it. If nothing bad happened he would seek out Sponger the next day. If nothing bad happened. For a moment he almost panicked. He crossed himself. God would not permit anything bad to happen. It was foolish to think of such a possibility. He would tell his story the next day, omitting his fear, and Sponger would be proud of him.

He turned the knob very slowly. Fortunately, the door was not locked. He became terrified again, but suddenly he conceived the curious idea that the danger lay elsewhere, that he could find sanctuary in the master bedroom. He went in, shut the door behind him, made a gesture of fatigue, breathed deeply, and assured himself that he was safe. His slight dizziness must have been caused by hunger. Really, a dope like him shouldn't take on such a job. Did he have the skill, the competence, for it? No, of course not. His talent was limited to entering houses through windows that had been left open, stealing whatever lay nearby, and beating it. That's all he was good for. His childish pride withered. If they discovered him, he wouldn't know which way to run. What troubled him at this moment, however, was less the fear of capture than the conviction of his own inadequacy. He knew he was going to fail: his hands would tremble, his joints would crack, he would knock over furniture.

He clasped his hands together in a sudden resolve to finish the job quickly. He fixed his attention on the big bed, where an elderly couple was sleeping. In alarm he fell to a crouch: if one of them woke up, he must not be standing there like a statue. Still bent over, he moved forward and hid behind the head of the bed, where he remained in the same position so long that he felt cramps in his legs. The windows were open, and the room was bathed in light from the street.

Turning his head he saw himself in the wardrobe mirror. He looked ridiculous, squatting there with his head twisted. He turned away from this disagreeable vision and noticed an arm hanging over the side of the bed. It was the arm of a lady, the sickeningly fat arm of a rich old lady. The hand was short and flabby, with rings on its plump fingers. He thought of trying to remove the rings with a bent needle. Sponger had taught him this trick, and he had some needles in his pocket. But he preferred not to take the chance. Sponger had iron nerves. To steal rings from a person's fingers! What a man! Years of practice, several prison terms.

On hands and knees he crawled to the wardrobe cabinet, opened it, and began to examine the clothes. He discovered a wallet, put it in his pocket, and hurried out into the hallway. At the door of the room where a light was on, he examined the contents of the wallet and found several banknotes. He tried to discern their amounts, but the light was insufficient.

He thought of leaving, took a few steps, and stopped. Sponger would ridicule him mercilessly for quitting before he had gone through the entire house. His terror had disappeared. He was amazed that he had come through all the danger without mishap. Of course he hadn't yet finished, but somehow he felt safe.

He opened one of the doors with a crowbar, lit his flashlight, and saw an oratory. What splendor! He wanted to take the beautiful images, especially the heavy, gold staff of Saint Joseph. He withdrew quickly, afraid of the temptation. He would never commit such a sacrilege.

He went into some of the other rooms and took various small objects of little value. He felt impelled to enter the room in which a light was on. There he could count his money. Besides, he wanted to be able to tell Sponger that he had gone there.

He managed to slip the doorbolt, went in, and hid behind a wardrobe cabinet. There was a narrow bed in the room, but he didn't look to see what manner of person was in it. He drew the wallet from his pocket and, for a time, stared like an idiot at its contents. He began to count the money, became confused, started again, and finally gave up. His fingers were trembling, the numbers were all jumbled together. He stuffed the bills into his trouser pocket. He would count the money later when he was calm. He would take it and go and live in a suburb where nobody knew him. He would quit this profession, for which he had no talent anyway, no talent at all. He wouldn't tell Sponger; he would avoid all such compromising characters. He would straighten himself out, become a respectable person, and start a business of some sort, far away from Sponger. Yes sir. He felt the bulge of the mass of bills and buttoned the pocket. He would become a decent person, yes sir, and this was the stuff that could do it for him.

He looked at the bed. At first he thought its occupant was a child, but then he saw an exposed breast. He trembled, turned away, and started toward the door. Then he stopped, turned again, and observed the young lady in the bed. He saw in her traces of the girl with the green eyes. His heart beat so violently in his narrow chest that it seemed about to leap out through his mouth.

He straightened up and averted his face. It was a crazy idea. He tried to think of ordinary, everyday things. He took a deep breath. He counted to ten. The tattoo on Sponger's leg was a horrible thing, really indecent. By now the café at the corner must be closed. He counted to ten again and exhaled. A fit of coughing interrupted these endeavors.

He hurried out of the room, making an enormous effort to keep silent. He needed air, tears were streaming from his eyes, the veins of his neck stiffened like taut ropes. He hurled himself through the hall and down the stairs, his hand in his mouth. He sat down on the lowest step and remained there several minutes, shaken by the stifled coughs. He began to wheeze softly, trying to get rid of a persistent tickle in his throat. He wiped away a trickle of saliva.

Gradually he recovered. Surely the people upstairs had awakened. He turned his head and cupped his ear. For a moment he had the mad notion that he could hear moths gnawing at the clothes in the cabinets. He should have taken some of the clothes; Sponger's fence would buy them.

He heard the sound of a whistle in the street and broke out in a sweat. A rooster crowed. Then everything was quiet again, except for some indeterminate little sounds, perhaps the patter of cockroaches' feet.

He got up, no longer terrified, and tried to take stock of his situation. He was hungry. The tickle in his throat had disappeared. Nonsense to listen to the cockroaches on the wall or to worry about the policeman's whistle in the street. These things had nothing to do with him; he was out of danger. Yes, out of danger. If his cough came back he would stifle it by biting his sleeve. He cleared his throat softly. Calm. Calm and hungry. He turned in one direction and then the other, torn between the little parlor and the pantry. The tickle in his throat had completely disappeared. His mouth filled with saliva. He listened: no policeman blowing his whistle, no rooster crowing, no cockroaches moving about. He wanted so much to go into the pantry. Now that he had recovered from his suppressed coughing and suffocation, he felt a need for refreshments.

He pressed the button on his flashlight. The weak light shone on the glass cupboard, then climbed up the table, dividing it in half. He placed the flashlight on the tablecloth. He drew the crushed bills from his pocket, bent over, and tried again to count the money. After several failures he finally thought he had the right sum. He considered it sufficient for the establishment of a bar in the suburbs. He smoothed the bills, folded them, put them back, and buttoned his pocket again.

He had capital now. He felt cold and hungry. The policeman must be dozing down at the corner by the café. He turned up his jacket collar. He had capital; he would establish himself in the suburbs as the proprietor of a café, far from Sponger and these dangers. A small, modest café with a radio and with decent customers, drinking and talking about soccer. This was where his talent lay. He would listen interestedly to the conversations without taking sides, he would never offend anyone, and he would see that his employees did their jobs properly. A boss, yes sir; he would treat his workers firmly but humanely. And Sponger wouldn't even recognize him if he saw him—stout, serious, working the cash register. Sure. He felt the lump of money and grew in strength. Fine. But no political intrigue in his café. Sports, inoffensive subjects, perfectly okeh; but whisperings, secret papers handed from one to another, absolutely no. Everything must be proper: no complications with the police.

He straightened up. A slight pain gnawed at his stomach. He took the flashlight and started for the pantry with the firmness and confidence appropriate to the proprietor of a tavern in the suburbs.

Suddenly he felt an overwhelming desire to laugh—softly, of course, lest he cough and gag again. He shook with this quiet laughter for several minutes, while his shadow danced on the floor. He had bungled everything from the start, he hadn't even known which doors were where, he had bounded noisily down the stairs—and no one had awakened. These people must sleep like corpses. So why be so careful, why take such precautions? Sponger knew how to work right, he even took rings off the fingers of people while they were asleep. A man of genuine accomplishment. And yet he had been arrested twenty times, had served several sentences, and had had any number of narrow escapes. So Sponger's knowledge and skill were really of little value. When God wants people to stay asleep, they stay asleep.

Where could the cheese be? He had seen it two days earlier on top of the refrigerator, but now he searched for it in vain. He went into the kitchen, looked in the casseroles, and found some pieces of meat, which he ate almost without chewing. His fingers were greasy from the fat and he licked them. Then, very deliberately, he turned on the water in the sink, washed his hands, and wiped them on his jacket. Relieved and satisfied, he breathed deeply. His light-headedness had entirely disappeared.

He thought of the clumsiness and stupidity with which he had handled the job. Holy Mary, what a bungler! If he told Sponger the whole story, with complete frankness, he'd have to listen to a sermon. But he wouldn't tell him anything. He wanted to have nothing more to do with Sponger. He was going to open a café in the suburbs.

He returned to the dining room and turned off the flashlight. The people upstairs must have been in a coma all this time.

A mad idea occurred to him: he would go up and down the stairs again, just to prove to himself that he was not so awkward as he seemed to be. Then the girl with the green eyes surged into his memory with one breast uncovered. Absurd. It was the young lady sleeping upstairs whose breast was uncovered. He wondered what the color of her eyes was.

The clock struck two, filling the house with the sound. The ticktock began to torment him. A few moments before, there was silence, but now the ticktock hammered inside his skull.

He returned to the parlor, tempted to go back into the rooms upstairs and take some additional objects to sell to the fence. He thought that by beginning again and, this time, following the rules expounded by Sponger, he might vindicate himself. The mass of bills, acquired so easily, now gave him no gratification.

He stepped on the first stair and trembled. The reasons for going upstairs fled his mind. Only the uncovered breast remained.

He tried to make himself think about the bar in the suburbs but couldn't. He stopped for a moment at the head of the stairs. "I must be crazy!" He went to the door of the room where the light was on, pushed it open, saw that the woman was still asleep.

And from that moment on, until the dreadful outcome, he didn't know what he was doing. The following day he remembered having stood a long time next to the bed, but he found it hard to believe he had done the mad act that brought about his downfall. How did it happen? It began with a sort of dazzlement. The house was spinning, the room was spinning, and he himself was spinning around the woman. He was a fly, circling, approaching, flying away. He had to light somewhere, to stop this dizziness. The image of Sponger came and quickly went; the eyeglasses of the man in the store and the panes of glass in the window of the house across the street, blended and faded away. The clock struck again, a whistle blew in the street, cocks crowed, and he heard all this; but it made no impression on him. And then came the disaster, the madness, the maddest of madnesses. He bent over and pressed a kiss on the young lady's lips.

The rest of the story is in the police records. Giddy, emotionally exhausted, he gives only fragmentary and contradictory information. In vain they question him, in vain they slap him around. All he knows is that he heard a scream of terror and then a noise in the other bedrooms. He remembers having gone down the hall and having taken one step on the stairs. He must have fallen down the stairway and lost consciousness. While he was falling he had a quick dream: he saw dirty cubicles crawling with bedbugs, pallets on the damp floor, horrible faces, gangs of prisoners carrying heavy beams. People were insulting him, raining blows on his back. But the insults faded away, the blows ended. And there was a long silence.

When he came to, he found many hands grasping him. Blood was flowing from a wound in his forehead. It got into his eyes, coloring everything and everyone red. An old man, wrapped in a blanket and holding onto the banister of the stairway, seemed to be gesticulating at him. And a woman's scream came from above, probably a continuation of the scream that had ruined his life.

*   *   *

GRACILIANO RAMOS (1892–1953) was born in Quebrângulo, Alagoas, and died in Rio de Janeiro. Manuel Bandeira, in his *Brief History of Brazilian Literature* (as translated by R. E. Dimmick), says of him: "He grew up in the backlands, at Palmeira dos Indios, went into business there, and eventually became municipal prefect. Moving to Maceió, he served as director of the State Printing Office, and later as Director of Public Instruction. A victim of repressive measures on the part of the police preceding the coup d'état of 1937, he was unjustly imprisoned and sent to the penal colony on the Ilha Grande. On regaining his freedom he took up residence in Rio, where he lived in near poverty as a secondary-school inspector and journalist, leaving only once, to make a trip to Russia. [He was an avowed Communist.] Pessimistic, austere in appearance, he nevertheless made many friends, and in his later years he was considered one of the masters of Brazilian fiction and prose style." Although he held public offices in education, Ramos himself never completed secondary school.

Two of Ramos's four novels have been published in English translation as *Anguish* and *Barren Lives*. Some consider his best works to be his prison memoirs, published posthumously, and a volume of childhood reminiscences.

"The Thief" ("Um Ladrão") is from his only book of short stories, *Insônia*, 1947.

Luís Jardim

The Enchanted Ox

Once (so the story goes) there was a ranch way up in the back-lands. The man who owned it was filthy rich. He had more than ten thousand head of cattle.

But this rancher also had a great fault: he was proud. He thought he was more important than the whole world, more important even than God. You could see his pride in the arrogant scowl he always wore. Everybody had to obey him and things always had to be done his way, even when he was wrong—which he would never admit. He was like a king: once he had spoken he never backed down.

One day, early in the afternoon, a dark brown ox—it was sort of mottled, really—appeared at the edge of the patio. This ox was so big that everyone was amazed.

The dogs barked and went after it, raising a flurry of dust. The rancher, who had his back to the patio, turned to see what the noise was all about.

"What monster of an ox is this!" he cried.

He called Tiúba, the cowboy who served as his personal helper, and asked:

"Tiúba, to whom does this ox belong?"

The cowboy said he didn't know. He said he had never seen such an ox before. It was frighteningly tall, taller even than the gate of the corral.

For seven days in a row, and always at the same time, the ox appeared in the patio. Each time, the dogs barked and ran at it, and the dust rose and hid them all.

The rancher became uneasy and suspicious. He knew the entire region, but he had never come across this ox or one anything like it. Being so proud, he decided he would have to capture the ox and own it, cost what it might. He waited impatiently for the ox to return.

He didn't have to wait very long, for the next day, at the same time, the animal was right there at the edge of the patio, digging at the ground with its hoofs.

The rancher shouted for Tiúba and ordered his horse to be saddled and brought to him as quickly as possible. It was a sorrel, beautiful, spirited, and as fleet as a deer. A horse so dreadfully wonderful that people called it Flyer.

Within a minute they brought the horse. Flyer pawed the earth and snorted, and the foam of rage dripped from its mouth. It was a fine animal, really fine. Its rump was round, shiny, and smooth as velvet. Just to look at such an animal was a delight. In its presence no one could even mention spurs; the horse wouldn't stand for it. Just a slight touch with the quirt; anything more and even a skilled horseman would find himself in the dust. Flyer had thrown the best of the cowboys, saddle and all. Let anyone ride it who dared!

Except its owner, of course. The rancher now mounted, placing his feet in the silver stirrups. Everything else was of silver too: the bit, the rein, even the quirt handle. Everything, everything of silver! Shining like a mirror.

Flyer was the most beautiful and the most handsomely equipped horse in that part of the country. Moreover, it was so strong and brave that it would attack the fiercest bullock and knock it down. The fame of the horse and of its owner spread everywhere. This just served to inflate the rancher's pride even more.

And so, with its master on its back, Flyer went prancing out into the patio. It didn't go straight forward; it went in circles like a peacock. Its tail, as clean and shiny as a young girl's hair, was so long that it trailed on the ground.

Now it galloped forward. Its hoofs beat a "pede*ray*, pede*ray*" on the hard earth, like the drumming of fingers on a table. The cloud it kicked up mingled with the rays of the sun and looked like gold dust.

When the rancher, crouched on his horse, reached the middle of the patio, he heard his wife calling his name. He turned and saw her motioning him to come back.

He clutched the rein, made a gesture as if to strike the horse, and off they went toward the house. What a sight! The horse didn't run, it flew. And the pebbles flew, too, under the impact of its hoofs.

On the terrace in front of the house, the rancher drew in the rein. The horse skidded to a stop, digging two furrows in the ground. It was a smart, sensitive horse, accustomed to stopping short right at the door.

Flyer's broad chest was bathed in sweat. The animal stood with one foot raised, like a bird. And you could tell what it wanted: to cut loose and chase after the brown ox. It did everything but say so. Its ears were erect, its head was down, and that broad, beautiful neck described a curve like the stick of a slingshot.

The rancher, all proud and haughty because he was richer and more powerful than anyone else, asked his wife what she wanted. She, in turn, asked where he was going, and he replied that it was none of her business. But then, beating his chest, he said:

"I'm going to catch that devil of an ox. It comes here and drives me mad. But today there is no saint in heaven that can save it from me!"

Then his wife, who was a fine woman, meek and good, said:

"All right, Lourenço"—that was the rancher's name—"All right, Lourenço, go. But put aside your pride and don't speak with such arrogance."

But he paid little heed, for he was more wrapped up than ever in his own importance. Not wanting to hear any more advice, he leaned over, close to his wife's face, and said:

"Listen: today I'm going to catch that ox, whether God wills it or not!"

He said this and galloped off. His wife could see little more than the horse's rear hoofs thrashing in the air.

Then the brown ox, which had been waiting at the end of the patio where the dogs were trying to keep it at bay, also set off. The dust was so thick you couldn't see exactly where they went.

In a short time that living cannonball—ox, horse, and rider—plunged into the scrub woods. It was like one great, mad beast. You could hear the snapping of branches. Trees and bushes seemed to be running past, as if they had feet too. Whistling like the wind. The chase left them all behind: red quebrachos, pepper trees, trumpet bushes. And the smaller plants underfoot were crushed into pulp.

The noise was loud and frightening. It was like the sound of a whirlwind during a drought. The great cloud of dust rose up to heaven like the smoke when trees and grass are burned for the clearing of a new field. There they went: the ox in front and the horse galloping after! the ox in front and the horse galloping after!

They leaped fences, they climbed mountains and came down the other sides, they dashed along the narrow trails of the woods. And, everywhere, they left behind a smooth path, as smooth as if it had been cleared with a scythe. Sometimes their hoofs would strike a melon cactus, and it would roll away like a three-banded armadillo tumbling down a hill.

After a while they came to a flat rock that was so wide you couldn't see the far edge of it. And the feet of the two animals struck fire on it. If you had been near, you would have smelled the burning hoofs and heard their crisp snap against the stone. Imagine the sound of popcorn over a fire, only much louder.

Well, when they got to the end of the rock, the rancher saw a great precipice. It was like the mouth of a dragon opened wide to swallow up everything. The precipice was so steep that any living creature crazy enough to try to walk down would surely get killed. It would slip and get smashed to pieces at the bottom. Not even a snake would try.

It was hopeless. So the rancher pulled his horse up short. Flyer was all soaked in sweat. It looked as if it had just taken a bath. Its nostrils were two chimney flues from which the breath blew with such force that it raised dust from the earth. Like bellows.

But the ox wasn't the sort of animal to be stopped by anything. Without hesitation it went right down the precipice and disappeared.

Down below there, it was dark as pitch. Blacker than coal. Not a ray of light could penetrate such depth.

Then the rancher stood up in his stirrups and leaned over the edge of the precipice. In a voice so loud that it could be heard all the way along the mountain range, he shouted:

"I didn't catch you, you monster, but at least I know you're dead! You'll never come out of there. Even the vultures won't be able to reach you. You'll never come onto my land again. Stay there and rot!"

Then the rancher slowly started back. Flyer, after its short rest, was eager to race again. No one would have believed it had run so far and so fast. Twisting its head, trying to get the rein in its teeth. But the rider, although more dead that alive, kept the horse firmly under control.

The ride had been rough on the rancher. His body was crazy tired. His face was all scratched, as if he had been fighting with a wildcat. Blood was trickling down and mixing with the sweat.

He felt very badly about the chase. It had failed, and the horse was to blame. Flyer was too heavy, its joints were rusty, it needed to exercise more. This was the first time an ox or any other animal had got away from the great horse.

But now everything was over. The rancher could relax in his hammock, knowing for sure that the ox was dead, down there at the bottom of the chasm.

When he got home, he told his wife what had happened, but he changed things. He boasted and said he had killed the ox in a valley. She didn't say a word.

The next day, early in the afternoon, the rancher's wife heard his voice thundering:

"Is it possible! There's that demon of an ox!"

And he began to shout for Tiúba.

The cowboy appeared in an instant. The proud rancher told him to bring the horse as quickly as possible. And, purple with rage, he screamed so that his wife would be sure to hear him:

"That animal won't get away today! I'll capture it or die! Where an ox can go, Flyer and I can go too!"

Even more quickly than the day before, Tiúba brought the horse, all saddled and ready. This time everything was of gold: the bit, the rein, the rings, the stirrups, everything. It was a joy to behold.

You could see that the horse was even more eager than the first time. It wouldn't stand still for anything. It was digging at the ground and making that sneezing sound, like a goat on a rainy day.

Then the rancher mounted and rode off like a flash. His wife called after him, but he cried:

"I won't listen to you! I know what you want. And it makes no difference to me whether I ride with God or the devil!"

His voice was drowned by the clatter of hoofs, and before long he and his horse disappeared in a cloud of dust.

This time the chase was even madder than the day before. The horse stayed right at the ox's heels. They leaped over gullies, clumps of cardoon, and clusters of wild pineapple. And from time to time a branch would slash like a razor, leaving strips hanging from the rancher's leather jacket.

On they dashed at breakneck speed. Flyer was running as if its life was at stake. Again and again it got within a few feet of the ox. But it could never eliminate that short distance. As if something was holding it back by the tail.

From time to time the rancher would try to encourage his horse. He would shout:

"You damned, stinking ox! You're bewitched! There's no animal in the world can catch you—except one, and that's my Flyer!"

The chase went on, headlong, pell-mell. Wherever they passed, the earth trembled and rocks rolled down the mountain slopes. The rough undergrowth flattened into a soft bed beneath the animals' hoofs.

Then the rancher heard a voice saying:

> "Tear the branches, press the hunt,
> Yet I will always be in front,
> And where I run you can't break through.
> God's beast am I, whose beast are you?
> Fly over stream, leap over rocks,
> You'll never, never catch the ox!"

And as a refrain, repeated at intervals:

> "You'll never, never catch the ox!
> You'll never, never catch the ox!"

Suddenly, Flyer stopped short. The rancher flew over the horse's head and sprawled face down on a bank of wild pineapple. It was like lying on a bed of nails. The prickles were so close together you couldn't get the head of a pin between them. The edge of every leaf had teeth like a handsaw.

When Flyer saw its master lying there and heard him groaning, groaning, it turned about and went straight back home. You would have thought it was trained, like a circus horse.

Tiúba was the first to see the horse—its bridle torn, its saddle empty. He spread the alarming news. All you could hear was crying, wailing, and hysterics. The rancher's wife, poor thing, carried on like a madwoman.

Then a party set out, with Flyer in front, to find the rancher. They went on and on and on. After a long time, when the sun had almost set, they found him, lying in the midst of the prickles, and his bellowing was enough to scare the daylights out of you—like a dog howling at the new moon.

They could hardly recognize the man, with the flesh of his face and body so dreadfully torn. They put him in a hammock and carried him home, like a lump of corn paste wrapped in a husk.

I don't know how many days he spent in bed, taking purple pine-seed medicine and washing his body with mimosa water to ease the pain. All I know is that he felt nervous and irritable because he was impatient to get going again. He would say:

"I'm safe from now on. If you have a narrow escape, you'll live a hundred years."

But Tiúba denied this. He said that if you have a narrow escape and take another chance, you're sure to get killed. And he said that what had happened was a punishment and that nobody could tell him otherwise.

After a long time, the rancher was well again and ready for another try. His pride was as bad as ever or maybe even worse than before. Worse, I think, for he was always frowning now with impatience to be first and foremost in everything. He spoke only in shouts, and the devil's name was always on his lips. And then, one afternoon, the ox appeared again.

The rancher hadn't told his wife about the voice he had heard. He felt absolutely sure the ox was bewitched. And when he saw the animal there at the far end of the patio, digging at the ground and sharpening its hoofs on a hard old mound made by termites, he came out of the house bellowing:

"Listen, you ox from hell! Today I'll take the curse off you or, by the devil, I'll die in the attempt!"

He shouted for Tiúba. When the cowboy came, the rancher was all ready. He had on his leather jacket and chaps, and his spurs were big enough to rip the horse's belly open. He gave Tiúba an order, and in a couple of minutes Flyer was ready too.

This time the trappings were the handsomest the rancher had. Full of the most beautiful stones in the world, stones of many colors. I don't even know the names of all of them. All I know is that each one cost a fortune and that the rancher had ordered them from countries far away, where there are princes and kings.

In the wink of an eye he jumped into the saddle. He rode off like an arrow and didn't even know whether his wife was calling after him or not.

When the ox saw the horse coming toward it like all hell broke loose, it knew what was up. I think it said:

"Legs, show me why I love you so!"

And it disappeared into the woods.

This chase was the wildest of all. Whatever they crashed into was destroyed. It was like the water when a dam bursts, wrecking everything in its way. And on they went ... here ... there ... but the ox always in front and the horse never catching up.

The rancher crouched down to avoid overhanging branches. The rein was loose, the horse could run as it pleased.

When they came near the place where the voice had spoken, the rancher shivered with fear from his head to his feet. A gentle wind hummed in his ear like the droning of a bee. And in a minute or two he heard the voice again:

> "Tear the branches, press the hunt,
> Yet I will always be in front,
> And where I run you can't break through.
> God's beast am I, whose beast are you?
> Fly over stream, leap over rocks,
> You'll never, never catch the ox!"

But this time the rancher expected the horse to stop short, and so he was all set and ready when it happened. He was badly shaken but not thrown. Dreadfully enraged, he buried his spurs in Flyer's belly. The horse groaned and cringed with pain. Then it leaped forward and followed the ox down into the chasm.

The rancher could smell death ahead. He felt certain that when they got so far down that there was no light at all, they would fall the rest of the way. It was so steep and so deep that not even an ant could have got safely to the bottom.

The woods were closing above them, at first like a fine sieve and then like a dense thatching which the sun could not penetrate. But the rancher thought:

"Wherever an ox can go, a rancher can go!"

When they could no longer see, in that moonless night, the rancher began to hear voices from all directions.

He was frozen with fear and expected momentarily to meet his death. Everything seemed to have come to an end: the woods, the stones, everything. Nothing was left in that darkness but a great, bottomless hole.

Then he heard a loud laugh as if someone was mocking him. And he thought:

"It must be a night hawk. They laugh just like people."

On they plunged headlong, not knowing where they were or where they were going. Farther on, the rancher heard a voice saying "cuckoo, cuckoo." And he thought:

"The cuckoo is an evil bird."

It was a bad omen. But he paid no heed and drove the spurs again into Flyer's belly.

The dark seemed boundless. It was like the end of the world. The rancher clung to the horse's mane to keep from falling.

And on they galloped. He heard voices again, and sometimes they seemed to be jeering or hissing. But he thought:

"These are saki monkeys climbing among the branches."

He heard a sound like pebbles being shaken in a box. But he thought:

"It is a rattlesnake creeping on the ground."

In a little while he heard something like the tearing of cloth. But he thought:

"It is the screech of an owl."

This was another bad omen. But the rancher paid it little mind, for if he succeeded in disenchanting the ox, surely all would go well with him.

Flyer's belly must have been oozing blood. The rancher was digging his spurs into it mercilessly, frantically, for he was afraid he would never get out of that endless tunnel.

From the midst of the darkness came a piercing cry. But the rancher thought:

"It must be a falcon calling to her mate."

A moment later he heard the sound of something moving on the ground. But he thought:

"It is a lizard running over the dry leaves."

Something beat lightly against his face, making a cold wind as it passed. But he thought:

"It is a guan and we have frightened it."

And so they continued the interminable chase. The rancher didn't know in what direction they were going or whether they were climbing or descending. He wondered if he had gone blind. All he knew was that he would never get out of that great hole and within an hour at the most he would be dead. Of this the rancher was certain.

But at last, far ahead, a thin shaft of light came through the foliage. Yes, at their swift pace they would soon emerge from the darkness and the sun would shine again.

And it happened exactly so. They suddenly came into a clearing, and the sun appeared there in the sky, making everything clear and bright. The rancher, more dead than alive, was still clinging to Flyer's neck.

When he looked about him, he saw that they were going around a curve in the road. Running ahead of them was a huge ostrich. But the ox was nowhere to be seen. Surely it had been spirited away, back there in the darkness.

The rancher, utterly exhausted, brought the horse to a stop. Flyer was black with sweat, and blood dripped from the slashes torn in its belly by the spurs. Even so, it did not take its eyes off the ostrich, which was disappearing into the woods.

The horse's trappings were ripped to pieces, and only two or three of the precious stones were still there. The twigs and branches of the trees had torn everything. The rancher's chaps and leather jacket were in shreds. One of his spurs had fallen off. His leather hat was gone. All scratched and bleeding, the poor rancher looked like the lowest kind of derelict.

Then, from the top of a tall brauna tree, a parrot said:

"O rancher, take heed:
God's in the lead,
Next comes the beast,
And you are the least."

The rancher looked up and saw the parrot. Its beak was golden, and its feathers were as beautiful as those of a peacock. Each of a different color, like the rainbow.

The rancher sat there on his horse, thinking, thinking. Then he dismounted and went over to a pond at the side of the road. He washed his face and cleaned the scratches on those parts of his body that were exposed. Indeed, as his clothes were in tatters, there was not much of him unexposed. Then he drank from the pond and let his horse drink.

He hadn't noticed how late it was getting. The sun was going down. The rancher sat on a stone to rest a little. He looked so sad you would have felt sorry for him. His head was lowered, and he was making marks in the dirt with a stick. He didn't notice the ants passing between his feet like a crowd of tiny people.

The rancher remained there a long time, thinking about God-knows-what. As if he had left the world and had forgotten it.

Someone touched him on the shoulder. He turned and saw a little old woman. He didn't ask who she was or where she came from. Not a word. He just sat there.

Then she spoke and said:

"Why are you so sad, cowboy?"

The rancher told her most of what had happened. But he didn't tell her that he had heard voices and that the parrot had talked to him, for he was ashamed to confess these things. Besides, he was afraid the old woman might be a witch.

She asked whether he had told her everything. He nodded his head. She laughed, for she knew that although his story was true it was not the whole truth. And then she consoled the rancher, saying:

"It doesn't matter, my son. Just have patience and, God willing, you'll catch the little calf."

The rancher was about to ask a question, but the old woman would not be interrupted:

"Whoever catches the calf—so the parrot with the golden beak tells me—will never lack cattle in his corral. Milk will flow from his cows like a river. And they will have as many heifers as there are trees in the backlands. There will always be plenty of rain on his land. Corn and beans and whatever else he may plant will grow abundantly. But only if God is willing."

Again the rancher wanted to ask a question. He thought he might not have heard aright. But when he turned around, the old woman was gone.

There was nothing more the rancher could do, so he mounted Flyer and rode off. He bestrode his horse as heavy-limbed as a ground hog. He was utterly depressed. Nothing can be compared to his sadness.

On and on they went, and the way seemed endless. The rancher paid no attention, however, to the road. He was mulling something over in his head:

"What a strange world this is! I am great and powerful, the owner of a wonderful horse, and to me the ox is a monstrous, enchanted beast that my horse cannot catch. Yet to the old woman, a weak and decrepit nothing of a person, the ox is just a little calf. She talks as if it was a pet you could lead around on a leash."

Flyer no longer seemed like a fine horse. So crippled and exhausted it couldn't even manage a slow trot.

It was late at night when they arrived back at the ranch. Everyone was waiting up, fearful that something terrible had happened. The rancher was so tired he could not dismount without help. His workers had to take him in their arms and lift him from the saddle.

From that day on, he remained in a pitiful state of depression. No one could get a word from him, not even a "good morning." He was morose, silent, separated from everyone like a chicken with the pip.

The rancher's story spread everywhere. And the fame of the enchanted ox grew greater and greater. All the ranchers and cowboys in the region wanted to capture the animal and break its enchantment.

And one day they all got together for that purpose. They

came from every direction in endless streams, riding the finest horses.

They went to the house of the proud rancher to get information, especially about the course the ox had taken. He came to the door and invited them to be his guests for the night. The next day he would give them all the information he had.

They accepted his invitation. In the evening, each of them told the most amazing story he had heard about the ox. The elder cowboys maintained that the ox was more than a hundred years old. No one had ever been able to catch it. Some had heard that only a cowboy who never had an evil thought could capture the ox. But they all agreed that to find such a cowboy would be the most difficult task in the world.

They got up early in the morning and prepared for their hunt. The ranch owner was not content merely to show them the ox's trail and tell them about the roads. He wanted to go along, and he tore his hair because he had no horse fit for such an ordeal. Flyer was no good any more; it had no appetite and was thin and dispirited.

Nevertheless, he decided to have Tiúba get the old sorrel ready. When Tiúba brought the horse, everyone roared with laughter. Flyer was just a skinny old plug, lame in one leg and sparse of mane. Its back, where the saddle would rest, appeared eaten away by lice.

The animal's disposition had changed completely. It was so gentle now that a child could ride it. It lacked the spirit even to whisk away the flies with its tail.

At the rancher's order they saddled the poor horse, which groaned under the weight as if the saddle had been made of lead. This time there were no precious stones and no trappings of silver or gold. Just an old leather bridle that Tiúba had put together. No one would have dreamed that this was the horse known as Flyer a short time before.

The rancher mounted carefully, afraid that the animal might collapse under the weight. He could hear the cowboys ridiculing the horse:

"That old nag couldn't catch a frog."

"Put me on a turtle and I'll race it."

"I'll bet I could get down on my hands and knees and beat it from here to the stable. Any takers?"

The rancher heard and didn't utter a peep. He was so sad it was pitiful.

When all was ready, they set out. There were so many ranchers and cowboys they almost filled the patio. Each had a horse more beautiful and fiery than the others. They frisked and leaped and raced one another. Noisy and wild like a bunch of demons or like a flock of macaws in a corn field.

And jogging behind came Flyer with the rancher on its back. It looked like an old pack mule.

The cowboys had forgotten about Flyer. Except once in a while when one of them would look back and say something like:

"Don't worry about the old nag. It's staying behind to pick up any cruppers that fall off."

"Nothing that ambitious," another would comment. "It just came along to feed the vultures."

And the poor rancher said nothing.

On and on they went, but there was no sign of the ox. At noon they rested under a hog-plum tree. Its trunk rose as high as the clouds, and its branches extended so far on every side that it was like a house. It could have shaded twice as many men.

Then (so the story goes) they heard a beating of wings. And in a few seconds they saw a parrot alight on a branch of the tree.

It was the parrot with the golden beak. The bird laughed merrily and said:

"Tell me, who'll catch the ox?"

At that very moment what should come along but the enchanted ox itself! It pawed the earth, sharpening its hoofs, and its eyes shone like two torches.

As soon as the cowboys recovered from their astonishment, they leaped on their horses and charged the ox. The earth trembled under the stampede. I can't describe how it was. Just imagine for yourself: all those horses rushing through the woods after a wild ox.

The only horse that did not join the chase was Flyer. It seemed to be nailed to the ground. The rancher thought of using the spur, but he knew it would do no good. The horse couldn't catch a sloth, let alone an ox like that.

The rancher felt miserable. He watched the red leather jackets disappear in the woods, and tears began to fall, one by one, from his eyes.

The parrot, up there in the tree, shook its feathers of many colors and cried:

"How about you, my proud friend! Aren't you going to catch the ox?"

Then the tears really flowed from the rancher's eyes. It would have broken your heart to see him.

After a while he looked up, but he could see almost nothing through his tears. Nevertheless, he replied to the parrot:

"Only if God wishes. . . ."

At that moment, without the rancher knowing how or why, Flyer suddenly became its old fiery self and set off at such a fearful speed that, if the rancher hadn't been a fine horseman, he would have been thrown and smashed to pieces.

Flyer's feet didn't touch the ground: they flew like doves. Never had an animal run so fast. Horse and rider flashed through the woods like lightning, leveling everything in their way.

In a large clearing they caught up with the cowboys. Flyer went past them so fast they didn't even recognize the horse. Anyway, how could they possibly have imagined that this could be Flyer!

Then the ox really extended itself, with Flyer just a short distance behind. They ran and they ran, and after a time they reached that great flat rock. All you could hear was the sharp noise of hoofs against stone. It was enough to split your eardrums. The sparks flew like those from a blacksmith's hammer.

Soon they came to the precipice and went down into the dark woods below. The other ranchers and cowboys, afraid to follow, took another route.

In the coal-black darkness of the chasm, the rancher began to hear the voice again. But this time it was saying:

"Mend the branches, end the hunt,
And who was last shall be in front.
You've found the key, you've broken through.
God's beast am I, God's man are you.
You've crossed the stream, you've crossed the rocks,
You'll catch the wild, elusive ox."

Then the horse really ran. No spur or whip was needed this time. The ground must have been made of velvet, for no noise was heard. The only sound was the breathing of the ox and the horse.

Then came the other voices. One kept saying:

"Repent! Repent!"

But the rancher thought:

"This is a bellbird singing."

Farther ahead he heard another voice:

"If God wishes, I wish. If God wishes, I wish."

But he thought:

"This is surely the song of a sparrow."

And galloping, galloping, he heard far below:

"Catch it, catch it, you will catch it! Catch it, catch it, you will catch it!"

But he thought:

"No doubt about it, that's a spine-tail singing."

Lightning itself could not have passed them, so swiftly they ran. And soon they spied a gleam of light. They had gone through the black woods in less than a minute. Before long, they came into that same clearing as the other time. The sun was so bright it hurt the rancher's eyes.

Right in the middle of the clearing, dominating everything, stood the brauna tree. And there at its top perched the parrot with the golden beak.

And when, in full chase, they passed under the tree, the rancher heard the parrot's voice again:

> "Below God,
>   Above beast,
> Rancher is
>   No longer least."

Then the horse began to tire. Now and again it stumbled and almost fell. The spurs dug into its belly and it leaped forward, but after a few yards its strength began to fail again.

The rancher knew that old Flyer would have to give up the chase. There was no remedy for it, the ox would escape forever.

But the rancher remembered the little old woman, and he thought:

"If God wanted me to, I could still catch the ox, even if I rode a turtle."

Flyer slowed down from a run to an ordinary gallop and then to a trot. There was no hope; the rancher would have to let the others catch the ox, if they could.

But then he observed that the ox was getting smaller and smaller. The slower the horse went, the smaller the ox became.

Soon Flyer slowed down to a limping jog. A person on foot could easily have kept up with it. And the ox went on shrinking, shrinking, until it was about the size of a steer.

When Flyer finally stopped altogether, the ox had become a calf. A tiny calf that any little boy could catch. As gentle as a house pet.

The rancher threw himself upon it, seizing the animal by its ears. They were as tender and soft as two *sacatinga* leaves.

Then the rancher thought of the old woman. Now he knew why she had called the ox a little calf. For it really was a calf, although an enchanted one.

When the other ranchers and the cowboys got there, they could hardly believe what they saw.

That's all that happened, except that the rancher became even more prosperous than before. No one has ever been able to count all his cattle. And they say—I don't know whether it's true—that whatever he plants grows a bumper crop every year.

One thing I know for sure is that, from that day on, the rancher never said he would do anything without adding "God willing." And two things he lost forever. One he was glad to lose and thanked God for taking from him: his pride. But the other, his eyes still fill with tears when he thinks of it: his horse Flyer, which died.

* * *

Luís Inácio de Miranda Jardim was born in 1901 in Garanhuns, Pernambuco. In 1918 he moved to Recife, the state capital, where he worked as a sales clerk but made friends in intellectual and

artistic circles. About 1936 he moved to Rio de Janeiro. There he
has occupied editorial posts in government agencies and with a large
publishing house. He is well known as an illustrator of books.

Luís Jardim has written fiction in various forms for both adults
and children. One of his books for children was published in English translation as *The Armadillo and the Monkey*.

"The Enchanted Ox" ("O Boi Aruá") is from the book *O Boi
Aruá,* 1940.

Antônio de Alcântara Machado

Gaetaninho

"Gaetaninho,* what are you doing there!"

He was day-dreaming right in the middle of the street. He didn't see the Ford that almost hit him. He didn't hear the dirty word the driver shouted at him.

"Hey, Gaetaninho! Come into the house."

It was a real motherly scream: a deaf child could have heard it. He turned his face, homely with freckles. He saw his mother and saw the slipper in her hand.

"Hurry up!"

He started toward her slowly, slowly. Frowning a little. Studying the terrain. Just in front of his mother he stopped. He swayed a little. A trick of the soccer champions. He moved slightly to the right. Then he suddenly did a half turn and darted to the left through the door.

Boy, a perfect feint!

When the people there on Orient Street rode at all, it was in a streetcar. Automobiles and coaches were only for a funeral. A funeral or a wedding. That is why Gaetaninho's dream had never come true. Just a dream.

Take Beppino, for example. That afternoon he got a ride across town to Araçá in a coach. But how? By being in his Aunt Permetta's funeral procession. That was about the only way. Patience.

Gaetaninho buried his head under the pillow.

Boy, what a deal! In the front, four black horses with plumes were hauling Aunt Filomena to the cemetery. Then came the

---

* Diminutive of the name Gaetano.

priest. Then came Savério, her fiancé, with his handkerchief to his eyes. Then came Gaetaninho. Up on the box, next to the coachman. In his sailor suit and white cap with the words *São Paulo Dreadnought* on it. No. The sailor suit was fine but instead of the cap he would wear the new straw hat his brother had brought him from the factory. And black garters on his stockings. What a deal, boy! Inside the coach his father, his two older brothers (one in a red necktie, the other in a green necktie), and his godfather Mr. Salomone. Lots of people on the sidewalks, in the doorways, and at the windows of the fine houses, watching the procession. Especially admiring Gaetaninho.

But Gaetaninho was not completely satisfied. He wanted to hold the whip. The coachman was mean and wouldn't let him. Not even for a few seconds.

Gaetaninho was going to holler but Aunt Filomena woke him up, singing *Oh Marie,* as she did every morning.

At first he was disappointed. Then he almost wept with hatred.

Aunt Filomena had an attack of nerves when she learned about Gaetaninho's dream. In fact, the whole family was alarmed at the bad omen. Gaetaninho felt remorse. To put their minds at rest, he decided to replace his aunt with someone else in a new version of the dream. He pondered, pondered, and finally chose the Gas Company's lamplighter, Mr. Rubino, who once had given Gaetaninho a rap on the head with his knuckles.

His brothers (wouldn't you know it) found some occult reason in the dream for picking a certain number to bet on in the numbers game. They lost and kicked themselves for not having seen that the actual winning number was the one that followed more logically from the dream.

The soccer game on the sidewalk seemed like a matter of life and death. Even though Gaetaninho wasn't paying attention.

"Did you know Afonso's father, Beppino?"

"My father once socked him in the face."

"Then they won't ask you to the funeral tomorrow. I'm going."

Said Vicente, indignant:

"I'm not going to play any more. Gaetaninho is goofing off."

Gaetaninho went back to his position as goalkeeper. So full of responsibilities.

Nino came toward him, dribbling the ball. He got very close. With his body arched, his knees bent, his arms extended, his hands open, Gaetaninho was all set for defense.

"Pass to Beppino!"

Beppino took two steps and kicked the ball. With all his might. It went over the freckled goalkeeper's head and rolled to the middle of the street.

"That's a hell of a kick!"

"Shut up, bigmouth!"

"Get the ball!"

Gaetaninho ran after it. Before he reached the ball a streetcar hit him. Hit him and killed him.

Gaetaninho's father was in the streetcar, coming home.

The kids were frightened. In the evening they spread the news.

"You know Gaetaninho?"

"What about him?"

"He got run over by a streetcar!"

The neighbors took out their Sunday clothes and cleaned them with benzine.

At four o'clock the next afternoon, the funeral procession started out from Orient Street and Gaetaninho was not on the coachman's box of any of the carriages in the train. He was up front in a closed coffin covered with inexpensive flowers. He had on his sailor suit and garters but not the straw hat.

There was a boy on the coachman's box of one of the carriages in the little procession. It was Beppino, wearing a proud, dazzlingly red suit.

✴   ✴   ✴

ANTÔNIO DE ALCÂNTARA MACHADO (1901–1935) was born in São Paulo and died in Rio de Janeiro. At the age of 19, while still a law student (he was graduated in 1923), he began his journalistic activities. These were to range from literary criticism and a column on the theater to articles on his European travels and, in 1933, the direction of a line of newspapers for municipalities in the interior of the state of São Paulo. Closely associated with the modernist movement, Alcântara Machado also contributed to, and in some cases helped to direct or edit, the new periodicals of the 1920's and early 1930's.

As a consequence of the Revolution of 1932, he went into politics and moved to Rio de Janeiro. Shortly before his untimely death, caused by peritonitis following an appendectomy, he had been elected to the federal legislature.

Alcântara Machado's literary reputation rests chiefly on his two books of short stories. Critics have remarked the directness of his style, his irony, and the Paulistano feeling of his work. He left an unfinished novel, which was published posthumously in the same volume with some stories not previously collected in book form. He also produced a learned monograph on Anchieta, the sixteenth-century Jesuit missionary known as the Brazilian apostle, and hoped some day to write a biography of him.

"Gaetaninho" is from *Brás, Bexiga e Barra Funda,* 1927.

Aníbal Machado

The Piano

"Rosália!" shouted João de Oliveira to his wife, who was up-stairs. "I told the guy to get out. What a nerve! He laughed at it. He said it wasn't worth even five hundred cruzeiros."

"It's an old trick," she replied. "He wants to get it for nothing and then sell it to somebody else. That's how these fellows get rich."

But Rosália and Sara looked somewhat alarmed as they came downstairs. The family approached the old piano respectfully, as if to console it after the insult.

"We'll get a good price for it, you'll see," asserted Oliveira, gazing at the piano with a mixture of affection and apprehension. "They don't make them like this any more."

"Put an ad in the paper," said Rosália, "and they'll come flocking. The house will be like *this* with people." She joined the tips of the fingers of her right hand in customary token of an immense crowd. "It's a pity to have to give it up."

"Ah, it's a love of a piano!" said João. "Just looking at it you think you hear music." He caressed its oaken case.

"Well, come on, João. Let's put the ad in."

It had to be sold so that the little parlor could be made into a bedroom for Sara and her intended, a lieutenant in the artillery. Besides, the price would pay for her trousseau.

Three mornings later, the piano was adorned with flowers for the sacrifice, and the house was ready to receive prospective buyers.

The first to arrive were a lady and her daughter. The girl opened the piano and played a few chords.

"It's no good at all, mama."

The lady stood up, looked at it, and noticed that the ivory was missing from some of the keys. She took her daughter by the hand and walked out, muttering as she went:

"Think of coming all this distance to look at a piece of junk."

The Oliveira family had no time to feel resentment, for three new candidates appeared, all at the same time: an elderly lady who smelled like a rich widow, a young girl wearing glasses and carrying a music portfolio, and a redheaded man in a worn, wrinkled suit.

"I was here ahead of you," said the young girl to the old lady. "It doesn't really matter. I only came because my mother wanted me to. There must be plenty others for sale. But I'd just like to say that I was ringing the doorbell while you were still getting off the bus. We came in together but I got here first."

This rivalry for priority pleased the Oliveiras. They thought it wise, however, to break up the argument, so they smiled at everyone and offered them all coffee. The young girl went over to the piano, while the redheaded man stood at a distance and evaluated it with a cool eye. At this moment a lady entered holding a schoolgirl by the hand. They sat down distrustfully.

Suddenly the young girl began to play, and the whole room hung on the notes that she extracted from the keyboard. Off-pitch, metallic, horrible notes. The Oliveiras anxiously studied the faces of their visitors. The redheaded man remained utterly impassive. The others glanced at one another as if seeking a common understanding. The newly arrived lady made a wry face. The perfumed old lady seemed more tolerant and looked indulgently at the old piano case.

It was a jury trial and the piano was the accused. The young girl continued to play, as if she were wringing a confession from it. The timbre suggested that of a decrepit, cracked-voiced soprano with stomach trouble. Some of the notes did not play at all. Doli joined in with her barking, a bitch's well-considered verdict. A smile passed around the room. No one was laughing, however. The girl seemed to be playing now out of pure malice, hammering at the dead keys and emphasizing the cacophony. It was a dreadful situation.

"There's something you ought to know about this piano," explained João de Oliveira. "It's very sensitive to the weather, it changes a great deal with variations in temperature."

The young girl stopped abruptly. She rose, put on some lipstick, and picked up her music portfolio.

"I don't know how you had the nerve to advertise this horror," she said, speaking to João but looking disdainfully at Rosália as if she had been the horror.

And she left.

João said nothing for a moment. After all, the insult had been directed at the old piano, not at him. Nevertheless, he felt constrained to declare that it was a genuine antique.

"They don't make them like this any more," he said emphatically. "They just don't make them."

There was a long silence. The status of the piano had reached its nadir. Finally, the redheaded man spoke:

"What are you asking for it?"

In view of what had happened, João de Oliveira lowered substantially the price he had had in mind.

"Five contos," he said timidly.

He looked at everyone to see the effect. There was a silent response. Oliveira felt cold. Was the price monstrously high? Only the old lady showed any delicacy at all: she said she would think it over. But, through her veil of mercy, João perceived her decision.

As they all were leaving, a man about to enter stepped out of their way.

"Did you come about the piano?" asked one of them. "Well, you'll . . ."

But Oliveira interrupted.

"Come in," he said cheerfully. "It's right here. Lots of people have been looking at it."

The man was middle-aged, with a shock of grayish hair. He lifted the lid of the piano and examined the instrument at length. "Probably a music teacher," thought João.

The man did not ask the price. "Thank you," he said and left.

The house was empty again. Sara returned to her room. Rosália and João looked at each other in disappointment.

"Nobody understands its value," commented João sadly. "If I can't get a decent price for it, I'd rather not sell it at all."

"But how about Sara's trousseau?" said Rosália.

"I'll borrow the money."

"You'd never be able to pay it back out of your salary."

"We'll postpone the marriage."

"They love each other, João. They'll want to get married no matter what, trousseau or no trousseau . . ."

At this moment, Sara could be heard shouting from her room that she could not possibly get married without two new slips and so forth.

"The thing is," Rosália went on, "this house is about the size of a matchbox. Where can we put the newlyweds? We'll have to give up the piano to make room for them. Nobody nowadays has enough room."

Sara's voice was heard again:

"No, don't sell the piano. It's so pretty . . ."

"It's also so silent," interrupted her mother. "You never play it any more. All you ever play is the victrola."

She went to her daughter's room to speak further with her. Strange that Sara should talk like that. Rosália put the dilemma flatly:

"A husband or a piano. Choose."

"Oh, a husband!" replied Sara with voluptuous conviction. "Of course."

She hugged her pillow.

"So . . . ?"

"You're always against it, Rosália," shouted João de Oliveira.

"Against what?"

"Our piano."

"Oh, João, how can you say such a thing!"

The next day, as soon as he got back from work, João de Oliveira asked about the piano.

"Did any people answer the ad, Rosália?"

Yes, there had been several telephone calls for information about the piano, and an old man had come and looked at it. Also, the redheaded man had come again.

"Did any of them say anything about buying it?" asked João.

"No. But the two men who came to the house looked at it a long time."

"They did? Did they look at it with interest? With admiration?"

"It's hard to say."

"Yes, they admired it," said Sara. "Especially the old man. He almost ate it with his eyes."

João de Oliveira was touched. It was no longer a matter of

price. He just wanted his piano to be treated with consideration and respect, that's all. Maybe it wasn't worth a lot of money but it certainly deserved some courteous attention. He was sorry he hadn't been there, but what his daughter told him of the old man's respectful attitude consoled him for the contumely of the day before. That man must understand the soul of antique furniture.

"Did he leave his address, Sara? No? Oh, well . . . he'll probably be back."

He rose from his chair and walked around the old instrument. He smiled at it lovingly.

"My piano," he said softly. He ran his hand over the varnished wood as if he were caressing an animal.

No candidate the next day. Only a voice with a foreign accent asking if it was new. Rosália replied that it wasn't but that they had taken such good care of it that it almost looked like new.

"Tomorrow is Saturday," thought Oliveira. "There's bound to be a lot of people."

There were two, a man and a little girl, and they came in a limousine. The man looked at the modest house of the Oliveira family and considered it useless to go in. Nevertheless, he went to the door and asked the make and age of the piano.

"Thank you. There's no need for me to see it," he replied to João's insistence that he look at it. "I thought it would be a fairly new piano. Good luck . . ."

And he went away.

João was grief-stricken. Ever since he had inherited the piano he had prized it dearly. He had never thought he would have to part with it. Worst of all, no one appreciated it, no one understood its value.

No one, except possibly the fellow who came the next Wednesday. He praised the piano in the most enthusiastic terms, said it was marvelous, and refused to buy. He said that if he paid so low a price for it he would feel he was stealing it, and that João and Rosália were virtually committing a crime in letting this precious thing get out of their hands. Oliveira did not exactly understand.

"Does he mean what he says?" he asked Rosália.

"I think he's just trying to be funny," she replied.

"I don't know. Maybe not."

Rosália was the first to lose hope. Her main concern now, when her husband came home from work, was to alleviate his suffering.

"How many today?"

"Nobody. Two telephone calls. They didn't give their names but they said they'd probably come and look at it."

Her voice was calm, soothing.

"How about the redheaded fellow?"

"I'm sure he'll be back."

For several days no one came or telephoned. João de Oliveira's feelings may be compared to those of a man who sees his friend miss a train: he is sad for his friend's sake and he is happy because he will continue for a time to have the pleasure of his company. João sat down near the piano and enjoyed these last moments with it. He admired its dignity. He confided his thoughts to it. Three generations had played it. How many people it had induced to dream or to dance! All this had passed away, but the piano remained. It was the only piece of furniture that bespoke the presence of his forebears. It was sort of eternal. It and the old oratory upstairs.

"Sara, come and play that little piece by Chopin. See if you remember it."

"I couldn't, Papa. The piano sounds terrible."

"Don't say that," Rosália whispered. "Can't you see how your father feels?"

Whenever Sara's eyes lit on the piano, they transformed it into a nuptial bed in which she and the lieutenant were kissing and hugging.

For days and days no prospective buyer appeared. Nothing but an occasional telephone call from the redheaded man, as if he had been a doctor verifying the progress of a terminal case. The advertisement was withdrawn.

"Well, João, what are we going to do about it?"

"What are we going to do about what, Rosália?"

"The piano!"

"I'm not going to sell it," João shouted. "Those leeches don't give a damn about the piano; they just want a bargain. I'd rather give it away to someone who'll take good care of it, who knows what it represents."

He was walking back and forth agitatedly. Suddenly the expression of his face changed.

"Listen, Rosália. Let's phone our relatives in Tijuca."

Rosália understood his purpose and was pleased.

"Hello! Is Messias there? He went out? Oh, is this Cousin Miquita? Look . . . I want to give you our piano as a present. . . . Yes, as a present. . . . No, it's not a joke. . . . Really. . . . Right. . . . Exactly. . . . So it won't go out of the family. . . . Fine. Have it picked up here sometime soon. . . . You're welcome. I'm glad to do it. . . ."

After he had hung up he turned to his wife.

"You know what? She didn't believe me at first. She thought it was All Fools' Day."

Rosália was delighted. João walked over to the old piano as if to confer with it about what he had just done.

"My conscience is clear," he thought. "You will not be rejected. You will stay in the family, with people of the same blood. My children's children will know and respect you; you will play for them. I'm sure you understand and won't be angry with us."

"When will they come for it?" interrupted Rosália, eager to get the room ready for the bridal couple.

The next day Messias telephoned his relatives in Ipanema. Did they really mean to give him a piano? It was too much. He was grateful but they really shouldn't. When his wife told him, he could hardly believe it.

"No, it's true, Messias. You know, our house is about as big as a nutshell. We can't keep the piano here, and João doesn't want it to fall into the hands of strangers. If you people have it, it's almost the same as if it was still with us. Are you going to send for it soon?"

Several days went by. No moving van came. Mr. and Mrs. Oliveira thought the silence of their relatives in Tijuca extremely odd.

"Something's wrong. Telephone them, Rosália."

Cousin Miquita answered. She was embarrassed. The moving men asked a fortune for the job.

"I guess it's the gasoline shortage. . . . Wait a few more days. Messias will arrange something. We're delighted about getting the piano. We think of nothing else, Rosália."

This last sentence struck a false note, thought Rosália. After a week, João de Oliveira telephoned again.

"Do you want it or don't you, Messias?"

"João, you can't imagine how terrible we feel about this," came the stammered reply. "You give us a fine present and we can't accept it. They're asking an arm and a leg to move it here. And, anyway, we really have no room for it. We haven't even got enough room for the stuff we have now. We should have thought of this before. Miquita feels awful about it."

"In short, you don't want the piano."

"We want it. . . . But we don't . . . we can't . . ."

João de Oliveira hung up. He was beginning to understand.

"You see, Rosália? We can't even give the piano away. We can't even give it away."

"What can you do, João! Everything ends up with nobody wanting it."

After a few minutes of silent despondence, they were aroused by Sara, who interspersed her sobs with words of bitter desperation. Her mother comforted her.

"Don't worry, child. It'll be all right. We'll sell it for whatever we can get."

"I want it out right away, Mama. In a few days I'm to be married and my room isn't even ready yet. None of our things are in here. Only that terrible piano ruining my life, that piano that nobody wants."

"Speak softly, dear. Your father can hear you."

"I want him to hear me," she cried, with another sob. She wiped her eyes.

João de Oliveira slept little that night. He was meditating about life. His thoughts were confused and generally melancholy. They induced in him a fierce rage against both life and the piano. He left the house early and went to a nearby bar, where he talked with several men.

"What is my husband doing in a place like that?" Rosália asked herself. João was never a drinker.

Oliveira came back accompanied by a shabbily dressed Negro and two husky Portuguese in work clothes. He showed them the piano. They hefted it and said they doubted if they could handle it, just the three of them.

Rosália and Sara looked on in amazement.

"Have you found a buyer?" asked Rosália.

"No, wife. Nobody will buy this piano."

"You're giving it away?"

"No, wife. Nobody wants it even for free."

"Then what are you doing, João? What in the world are you doing?"

João's eyes watered but his face hardened.

"I'm going to throw it in the ocean."

"Oh, no, Papa!" exclaimed Sara. "That's crazy!"

The Oliveiras could not see the ocean from their windows, but they could smell it and hear it, for they were only three blocks from the avenue that ran along the beach.

The men were waiting, talking among themselves.

"What a courageous thing to do, João!" said his wife. "But shouldn't we talk it over first? Is there no other way out? People will think it funny, throwing a piano into the water."

"What else can we do, Rosália? Lots of ships go to the bottom of the ocean. Some of them have pianos on board."

This irrefutable logic silenced his wife. João seemed to take heart.

"Okeh, you fellows," he cried. "Up with it! Let's go!"

One of the Portuguese came forward and said humbly, on behalf of his colleagues and himself, that they couldn't do it. They hoped he would excuse them, but it would hurt their conscience to throw something like that in the sea. It almost seemed like a crime.

"Boss, why don't you put an ad in the paper? The piano is in such good condition."

"Yes, I know," replied Oliveira ironically. "You may go."

The men left. For a moment the Negro entertained the idea that he might take the piano for himself. He stared at it. He was fascinated by the idea of owning something, and a fine, luxurious thing at that. It was a dream that could become an immediate reality. But where would he take it? He had no house.

Rosália rested her head on her husband's shoulder and fought back the tears.

"Ah, João, what a decision you have made!"

"But if nobody wants it, and if it can't stay here . . ."

"I know, João. But I can't help feeling sad. It's always been with us. Doesn't it seem cruel, after all these years, to throw it in the ocean? Look at it, standing there, knowing nothing about what's going to happen to it. It's been there almost twenty years, in that corner, never doing any harm . . ."

"We must try to avoid sentimentality, Rosália."

She looked at him with admiration.

"All right, João. Do what you must."

Groups of Negro boys, ragged but happy, start out from the huts at Pinto and Latolandia where they live, and stroll through the wealthy neighborhoods. One can always find them begging nickels for ice cream, gazing in rapture at the posters outside the movie houses, or rolling on the sand in Leblon.

That morning a southwester was whipping the Atlantic into a fury. The piano, needless to say, remained as tranquil as ever. And imposing in the severity of its lines.

Preparations for the departure were under way. João de Oliveira asked his wife and daughter to remove the parts that might possibly be useful. Accordingly, the bronze candlesticks were taken off, then the pedals and metal ornaments, and finally the oak top.

"Ugh!" exclaimed Sara. "It looks so different."

Without mentioning it to his family, João de Oliveira had recruited a bunch of Negro boys. They were waiting impatiently outside the door. Oliveira now told them to come in, the strongest ones first.

It was twenty after four in the afternoon when the funeral cortege started out. A small crowd on the sidewalk made way for it. The piano moved slowly and irregularly. Some people came up to observe it more closely. Rosália and her daughter contemplated it sadly from the porch, their arms around each other's shoulders. They could not bring themselves to accompany it. The cook was wiping her eyes on her apron.

"Which way?" asked the Negro boys when the procession reached the corner. They were all trying to hold the piano at the same time, with the result that it almost fell.

"Which way?" they repeated.

"To the sea!" cried João de Oliveira. And with the grand gesture of a naval commander he pointed toward the Atlantic.

"To the sea! To the sea!" echoed the boys in chorus.

They began to understand that the piano was going to be destroyed, and this knowledge excited them. They laughed and talked animatedly among themselves. The hubbub inspired the little bitch Doli to leap in the air and bark furiously.

The balconies of the houses were crowded, chiefly with young girls.

"Mother of heaven!" they exclaimed. "What is it?" And, incredulously, "A piano!"

"It came from ninety-nine," cried a Negro urchin, running from house to house to inform the families.

"Why, that's where Sara lives."

"It's João de Oliveira's house."

An acquaintance ran out to learn the facts from Oliveira himself.

"What's wrong, João?"

"Nothing's wrong. I know what I'm doing. Just everybody keep out of the way."

"But why don't you sell it?"

"I'll sell it, all right. I'll sell it to the Atlantic Ocean. See it there? The ocean . . ."

With the air of a somewhat flustered executioner, he resumed his command.

"More to the left, fellows. . . . Careful, don't let it drop. . . . Just the big boys now, everybody else let go."

From time to time one of the boys would put his arm inside the piano and run his hand along the strings. The sound was a sort of death rattle.

A lady on a balcony shouted at João, "Would you sell it?"

"No, madam, it's not for sale. I'll give it away. You want it?"

The lady reddened, felt offended, and went into her house. João made his offer more general.

"Anyone around here want a piano?"

At number forty-three a family of Polish refugees accepted. They were astounded, but they accepted.

"Then it's yours," shouted João de Oliveira.

The Polish family came down and stood around the piano.

"We'll take it, all right.... But ... our house is very small. Give us a couple of days to get ready for it."

"Now or never!" replied Oliveira. "Here it is, right outside your house. You don't want it? Okeh, fellows, let's go."

The piano moved closer and closer to the sea. It swayed like a dead cockroach carried by ants.

João de Oliveira distinguished only a few of the exclamations coming from the doors, windows, and balconies of the houses.

"This is the craziest thing I ever heard of," someone shouted from a balcony.

"Crazy?" replied João de Oliveira, looking up at the speaker. "Okeh, then you take it. Take it. . . ."

Further on, the scene was repeated. Everyone thought it was a crazy thing to do and everyone wanted the piano; but as soon as the owner offered immediate possession, there was just embarrassed silence. After all, who is prepared to receive a piano at a moment's notice?

João de Oliveira proceeded resolutely, accompanied by a buzz of comments and lamentations. He decided to make no more replies.

A group of motorcycle policemen stopped the procession and surrounded the old piano. João de Oliveira gave a detailed explanation. They asked to see his documents. He went back to the house and got them. He thought the requirement natural enough, for the nation was at war. But he resented having had to give an explanation, for he was acting pursuant to a personal decision for which he was accountable to no one outside the family. He certainly had a right to throw away his own property. This thought reawakened his affection for the instrument. Placing his hand on the piano as if on the forehead of a deceased friend, he felt deeply moved and began to discourse on its life.

"It's an antique, one of the oldest pianos in Brazil."

It had belonged to his grandparents, who had been in the service of the Empire.

"It was a fine piano, you may believe me. Famous musicians played on it. They say that Chopin preferred it over all others. But what does this matter? No one appreciates it any more. Times have changed. . . . Sara, my daughter, is getting married.

She'll live with us. The house is small. What can I do? No one wants it. This is the only way out."

And he nodded toward the sea.

The Negro boys were growing impatient with the interruptions. They were eager to see the piano sink beneath the waves. Almost as impatient as these improvised movers, were the people who had joined the procession, including delivery men, messenger boys, a few women, and a great many children.

The police examined the interior of the piano but found nothing suspicious. They returned Oliveira's papers and suggested that he hurry so that traffic would not be impeded.

A photographer asked some of the people to form a group and snapped their picture. João de Oliveira was on the left side in a pose expressing sadness. Then he became annoyed with all these interruptions that prolonged the agony of his piano.

Night fell rapidly. A policeman observed that after six o'clock they would not be permitted to go on. They would have to wait till the next day.

The Negro boys dispersed. They were to be paid later, at Oliveira's house. People were amazed that evening at the number of young Negroes strolling around with small, ivory-plated pieces of wood in their hands.

The piano remained there on the street where they had left it, keeled over against the curb. A ridiculous position. Young men and women on their evening promenade soon surrounded it and made comments.

When he got home, João de Oliveira found some of Sara's girl friends there, eagerly questioning her about the piano.

It was still dark when João and his wife awoke to the loud sound of rain. Wind, rain, and the roar of the surf. They lit the light and looked at each other.

"I was thinking about the piano, Rosália."

"So was I, João. Poor thing! Out in the rain there . . . and it's so cold!"

"The water must be getting into the works and ruining everything . . . the felt, the strings. It's terrible, isn't it, Rosália."

"We did an ungrateful thing, João."

"I don't even like to think about it, Rosália."

João de Oliveira looked out the window. Flashes of lightning illuminated the trees, revealing branches swaying wildly in the wind. João went back to bed and slept fitfully. He woke again and told his wife that he had been listening to the piano.

"I heard everything that was ever played on it. Many different hands. My grandmother's hands, my mother's, yours, my aunt's, Sara's. More than twenty hands, more than a hundred white fingers were pressing the keys. I never heard such pretty music. It was sublime, Rosália. The dead hands sometimes played better than the live ones. Lots of young girls from earlier generations were standing around the piano, listening. Couples who later got married were sitting nearby, holding hands. I don't know why, but after a while they all looked at me—with contempt. Suddenly the hands left the piano, but it kept on playing. The Funeral March. Then the piano shut by itself. . . . There was a torrent of water. The piano let itself get swept along . . . toward the ocean. I shouted to it but it wouldn't listen to me. It seemed to be offended, Rosália, and it just kept on going. . . . I stood there in the street, all alone. I began to cry. . . ."

João de Oliveira was breathing hard. The mysterious concert had left him in a state of emotion. He felt remorseful.

The rain stopped. As soon as it was light, João went out to round up the Negro boys. All he wanted now was to get the thing over with as quickly as possible.

The wind was still strong, and the ocean growled as if it were digesting the storm of the night before. The boys came, but in smaller number than before. Several grown men were among them. João de Oliveira, in a hoarse voice, assumed command again.

On the beach the piano moved more slowly. Finally the long tongues of the waves began to lick it.

Some families stood on the sidewalk, watching the spectacle. Oliveira's crew carried and pushed the piano far enough for the surf to take charge and drag it out to sea. Two enormous waves broke over it without effect. The third made it tremble. The fourth carried it away forever.

João de Oliveira stood there, knee deep in water, with his mouth open. The sea seemed enormously silent. No one could tell that he was crying, for the tears on his cheeks were indistinguishable from the drops of spray.

Far off, he saw Sara with her head resting on the lieutenant's shoulder. Doli was with her, her snout expressing inquiry and incipient dismay; she always had slept next to the piano. João was glad that Rosália had not come.

Many people appeared later on the beach, asking one another what had happened. It seemed at first that an entire Polish family had drowned. Subsequently, it was learned that only one person had drowned. Some said it was a child. Others insisted that it was a lady who had had an unhappy love affair. Only later was it generally known that the person who had drowned was a piano.

People posted themselves at their windows to watch João de Oliveira come back from the beach.

"That's the man!" someone announced.

Oliveira walked slowly, staring at the ground. Everyone felt respect for him.

"It's gone, Rosália," he said as he entered the house. "It has passed the point of no return."

"Before we talk about it, João, go change your clothes."

"Our piano will never come back, Rosália."

"Of course it won't come back. That's why you threw it in the sea."

"Who knows," said Sara. "Maybe it'll be washed up on a beach somewhere."

"Let's not think about it any more. It's over. It's finished. Sara, it's time you did your room."

There was a pause, after which João resumed his lamentation.

"I saw the waves swallow it."

"Enough, my husband. Enough!"

"It came back to the surface twice."

"It's all over! Let's not think about it any more."

"I didn't mention it to anybody so they wouldn't think I went crazy . . . though they're beginning to think I'm crazy anyway. . . . The fact is, I'm probably the most rational man in the whole neighborhood. . . . But a little while ago I clearly heard the piano play the Funeral March."

"That was in your dream last night," Rosália reminded him.

"No, it was there by the sea, in broad daylight. Didn't you hear it, Sara? Right afterwards, it was covered all over with foam, and the music stopped."

He nodded his head, expressing hopelessness before the inevitable. He was talking as if to himself.

"It must be far away by now. Under the water, moving along past strange sights. The wrecks of ships. Submarines. Fishes. Until yesterday it had never left this room. . . . Years from now it will be washed up on some island in an ocean on the other side of the world. And when Sara, Rosália, and I are dead, it will still remember the music it made in this house."

He left the room. Sara, alone, looked at the place where the piano had been. Again, she pictured the conjugal bed there, but this time she felt a little guilty.

Her thoughts were interrupted by a knock at the door. A fellow came in with an official notice. Some unidentified person had told the police that a secret radio was hidden in the piano and that her father had wanted to get rid of it. He was to appear at the district police station and answer questions. Well, it was the sort of thing you had to expect in wartime. Nothing anyone could do about it.

Oliveira spent the rest of the day at the police station. He came home late.

"What a life, Rosália!" he said as he fell dejected into the armchair. "What a life! We can't even throw away things that belong to us."

João felt oppressed, stifled. He meditated awhile and then spoke again.

"Have you ever noticed, Rosália, how people hate to get rid of old things? How they cling to them?"

"Not only old things," replied Rosália. "Old ideas too."

Doli was sniffing the area where the piano had been. She wailed a little and fell asleep.

The doorbell rang. A man entered and drew some papers from a briefcase. He said he came from the Port Captain's office.

"Are you João de Oliveira?"

"Yes, I am João de Oliveira."

"What did you cast in the sea this morning?"

Oliveira was stupefied.

"Out here we're not in the port, my dear sir. It's ocean."

"Are you going to give me a vocabulary lesson, Mr. Oliveira?"

The man repeated his previous question and explained that regulations now forbade the placing of objects in or on the sea without a license.

"Have you a license?"

Oliveira humbly asked whether what he had done was in any way offensive or bad.

"That's not the question. Don't you know that we're at war? That our coasts must be protected? That the Nazis are always watching for an opportunity?"

"But it was just a piano, sir."

"It's still a violation. Anyway, was it really a piano? Are you absolutely sure?"

"I think I am," João blurted, looking at his daughter and his wife. "Wasn't it a piano, Rosália? Wasn't it, Sara?"

"Where's your head, João!" exclaimed Rosália. "You know it was a piano."

Her husband's doubt surprised everyone. He seemed to be musing.

"I thought a person could throw anything in the ocean that he wanted to."

"No, indeed! That's all we need. . . ."

João arose. He looked delirious.

"Suppose I want to throw myself in the sea. Can I?"

"It all depends," replied the man from the Port Captain's office.

"Depends on whom? On me and nobody else! I'm a free man. My life belongs to me."

"Much less than you think," said the man.

Sara broke into the smile with which she always greeted the lieutenant, who had just come in. She ran to kiss him.

"See our room, darling. It looks good now, doesn't it?"

"Yes, real good. Where are you going to put the new one?"

"The new one?"

"Yes. Aren't you going to get another?"

Sara and her mother exchanged glances of amazement.

"I'm crazy for a piano," said Sara's fiancé. "You have no idea how it relaxes me. All day long I have to hear guns shooting. A little soft music in the evening . . ."

Sara had a fit of coughing. João de Oliveira went out the door. He felt suffocated; he needed to breathe.

Who else would come out of the night and make new demands of him? How could he have known that a piano hidden from the world, living in quiet anonymity, was really an object of public concern? Why hadn't he just left it where it was?

It was miles away now, traveling. . . . Far away, riding the southern seas. . . . And free. More so than he or Sara or Rosália. It was he, João de Oliveira, who now felt abandoned. For himself and for his family. It wasn't their piano any more. It was a creature loose in the world. Full of life and of pride, moving boldly through the seven seas. Sounding forth. Embraced by all the waters of the world. Free to go where it wished, to do what it wished.

Beneath the trees in front of the house, the Negro boys were waiting for their second day's pay. They had worked hard. It was so dark that he could scarcely distinguish their shaved heads. In the midst of them he saw a vaguely familiar form. The person opened the garden gate and asked permission to enter.

With some difficulty João recognized the redheaded man, but he was wholly unprepared for what the man was about to say:

"I've come back about the piano. I think I can make you a reasonable offer."

✳   ✳   ✳

ANÍBAL MONTEIRO MACHADO (1895–1964) was born in Sabará, Minas Gerais, and died in Rio de Janeiro. He received a law degree and, in 1919, was appointed public prosecutor in a town in Minas. By temperament he was ill-suited to this position, which he held for only about a year; he resided in a building opposite the court house and, as he put it, "I always felt like taking the accused home for a cup of coffee." He subsequently became a high school teacher in Belo Horizonte. In 1923 he moved to Rio de Janeiro, where he held various public offices, each for a short period, and where, for a time, he taught literature in high school. After a period of indigence he became again a public official, thanks to the efforts of friends. His final twenty-five years were spent in Ipanema (a subdivision of Rio), where his house became a literary salon.

Aníbal Machado's contributions to periodicals had earned him a reputation long before the publication in 1944 of his first book, Vila Feliz, from which "The Piano" ("O Piano") is taken. He began a novel in 1926, worked on it intermittently for six years, then left it in a drawer for twenty-eight years, after which he completed it; it was published posthumously. He also wrote essays, prefaces, prose poems, and two plays, one of them based on "The Piano." Because of his perfectionism—and, perhaps, his carioca-like disposition—the output of his pen is more impressive in quality than in quantity.

Ribeiro Couto

The Bahian

The Legalist troops from Minas Gerais reached the county boundary and were thus only about two miles from São Bento. Although the revolutionary headquarters in São Paulo had assigned thirty police soldiers to the town, many families fled and moved down the mountain roads toward Pindamonhangaba. Rumor had it that the Mineiro soldiers cut off their prisoners' heads. The fugitives used every available vehicle: automobiles, trucks, ox carts. The pastures were empty; every horse had been pressed into service.

Old Captain Candinho went for his regular afternoon chat at Maximiano's store, but his cronies were not there. Maximiano himself had decided to shut up shop and to hide the merchandise in his country house. Let the Mineiros take São Bento; they would never eat any of his beans!

Judge Calimério telegraphed to São Paulo: he explained the desperateness of the situation, stated that almost all the court employees had fled, and asked for instructions. A member of the revolutionary cabinet sent an impudent reply:

"Stay there and uphold the majesty of the law."

This message disturbed the austere magistrate more than the civil war itself, the war that was bloodying the State and terrifying this usually tranquil mountain town.

From the cemetery hill one could see the trenches in which the Paulistas were defending the territory against the invading Mineiros. Colonel Faria, the local political boss, had not fled; he spent most of the day on the hill, following the operations through his binoculars. When the shots rang out and echoed through the mountain valleys, he wept with rage and shook his fist.

"You wait, you traitorous gang of Mineiro cutthroats! You'll get paid for this!"

His daughter, Iaia Faria, had organized the Red Cross in the Municipal Council building. The town's charity hospital had only four beds and they were occupied by two soldiers and two civilians. The other wounded were accommodated on straw pallets in the rooms of the council building. On the walls they could read the official announcements, ineffective now except as reminders of the seemingly remote days when peaceful sessions of the council were held there, with debates about taxes and projects for town improvements.

So far, only one man had died in the fighting at the boundary: a little Negro private first class, shot through the eye. When his body was brought to São Bento, everyone came out to honor the hero. There was an elaborate funeral, including a speech by Colonel Faria. The young ladies of the Red Cross covered the grave with flowers.

The lieutenant in charge of the troops sent one telegraph message after another to the headquarters in São Paulo explaining that the Mineiros were receiving reinforcements and that they would soon attack São Bento. Its capture would give the Legalist forces access to the road leading to Pindamonhangaba, by which road they could go down to the valley of the Paraíba River. Thus they could cut off the rear guard of the Paulista forces moving against Barra do Pirai.

The high command then sent fifty volunteers, young athletes from Santos who rowed in the regattas. They marched down the main street of São Bento, exhibiting their fine physiques. Now the Mineiros were in for it, all right!

Colonel Faria wept with enthusiasm, and Iaia fell in love with one of the volunteers but wasn't sure which one.

João Estafeta was a thin, short, sickly backwoodsman. No one had supposed him capable of anything worthwhile. Now João Estafeta was a spy. He risked his life every day to obtain information for the Paulistas. Disguised as a muleteer, he would move along the mountain trails and penetrate the enemy's lines. On the night the volunteers from Santos arrived, he showed up in São Bento and announced:

"The Mineiros are expecting reinforcements too—a battalion from Bahia."

Bahians! Everyone knew their reputation for cruelty. Their troops were recruited from bandits, murderers, and backwoods vagabonds. The Governor of Bahia put uniforms on them and sent them south on ships to help the federal government.

That night, the few families that had remained in São Bento were unable to sleep, for they were terrified. Early in the morning, the sound of shooting brought the curious to the cemetery hill. A fierce battle was raging at the boundary.

"They're going to come in!" sobbed Maximiano.

"Never, never!" snarled Judge Calimério, looking through his binoculars.

"They won't take São Bento, the cutthroats!" roared Colonel Faria.

The rat-tat-tat of the machine guns sounded like hail on a tin roof. Hand grenades exploded with a dry sound. The soldiers could be seen running, protected by the trenches, changing position.

"That one died," shouted Judge Calimério, handing the binoculars to Colonel Faria.

The shots were now distinctly spaced. Then silence. Through the calm that pervaded the valley of the Sapucaí, the wind carried delirious hurrahs. And, strange to this region, the reverberation of a chant:

"Allagwa gwa gwa! Allagwa gwa gwa!"

It was, of course, the team yell of the oarsmen from Santos. Colonel Faria hurried down the hill in an ecstasy of joy.

Escorted by five Paulista soldiers, the Bahian reached Aterrado Bridge at the edge of the town, near the old walls of Colonel Faria's estate. Many people, informed that the Paulistas had taken a prisoner, were waiting ahead to see him go by. Was he a bandit? a murderer? After all, what would you expect a Bahian to be?

The escort, commanded by a corporal, crossed the bridge and moved on. In the front was the prisoner, wearing a torn khaki shirt. A mulatto with a week's growth of beard. He walked calmly, obviously tired, and with no show of arrogance.

The prisoner looked commonplace enough. But João Estafeta told everyone that he was ferocious, that he had hurled himself at the Paulista trenches with bayonet set, trying to force a way for his more cautious companions, who were held off by hand grenades. Suddenly he had found himself surrounded by Paulista soldiers. He had merely said:

"All right, I lose."

And he had surrendered.

The escort proceeded down Aterrado Street toward the Square of the Matriz, so that the entire city could see the prisoner. All of the families, without exception, that had not fled and had not gone out into the street, were at the windows. They looked at the prisoner with mingled curiosity and hatred. So this was the wretched, miserable Bahian!

As they were passing a bar, the prisoner stopped and said to the escort:

"Friends, would you buy me a pack of cigarettes?"

And he drew a coin from his pocket.

The corporal hesitated. One of the soldiers said:

"There's no harm in it, Corporal."

The corporal told the soldier to go ahead and buy the cigarettes. The prisoner opened the pack and offered cigarettes to the members of the escort.

A murmur spread among the people in the street. Antoninho Bilheteiro yelled:

"Let's lynch this impudent Bahian!"

Other voices took up the cry:

"Lynch him! Lynch him!"

The corporal raised his hand in token of silence, and one could see that he was saying "sh." But the people were excited now and continued to shout as they accompanied the Bahian and the soldiers to the Square of the Matriz. There the escort took its prisoner down the little street leading to the jail.

The jail was guarded by three local civilians: Pedro Parente, a clerk in the revenue office, who was armed with a revolver; Neco Emerenciano, a court employee, who had a Mauser; and the regular jailer, with a hunting rifle.

When the prisoner had been handed over to these gentlemen, the corporal turned to the people in the street and said loudly and distinctly, as if he were making a speech:

"Prisoners are sacred. Remember that. If any of you are looking for violence, go and fight in the trenches."

The people felt embarrassed. They dispersed. The escort marched back whence it had come, to the enthusiastic applause of the families at the windows. The five Paulista soldiers disappeared up the road in the direction of the fighting.

The plot was hatched by Antoninho Bilheteiro. A group of ten men, with the complicity of the three guards, took the Bahian out of the jail. They would "teach him a good lesson."

It was late afternoon. The shooting at the boundary had begun again. The Legalists were renewing their attack, determined to break through to the road leading into the Paraíba valley.

But the people paid little attention to the sound of the distant machine guns, which were like invisible motorists in an endless race. A crowd surrounded the Bahian, whom Antoninho Bilheteiro was leading in triumph toward Aterrado Bridge. The window shutters were quickly closed so that the young girls would not see the prisoner. His hands were tied behind his back, and he was nude except for a canvas sack tied around his middle. Voices screamed with anger:

"Tear him to pieces, the murderer!"

"Dog!"

"You'll see what Paulistas are like, you stinking Bahian!"

Dusk seemed to clothe the mulatto. With his head lowered, his stubby beard touching his chest, he appeared resigned and indifferent to the shouts of the crowd.

"What's your name, you Bahian bum?"

"Speak, Negro!"

Shoving one another in their bloodthirsty eagerness, the crowd followed close on the heels of the triumphant Antoninho Bilheteiro and his prisoner.

When they got to the bridge, Antoninho Bilheteiro clapped for silence.

"Listen, everybody! The people of São Bento have condemned this Bahian to death. It has been decided that he will die by drowning in the Sapucaí River."

The Bahian faced death calmly. It was night now and the dim street lights looked on the prisoner with compassion. The people pushed the mulatto to the edge of the bridge. Below swirled the waters of the river.

João Estafeta knew the value of a prisoner as a possible source of the kind of information for which he risked his life. Therefore he announced that he would interrogate the Bahian. The people waited anxiously.

"Bahian," he said softly, "we'll spare your life if you tell us straight everything you know about the Legalists."

Maximiano, who had just closed his store, came running to take part in the execution. People were beginning to wonder whether the lynching was really going to take place or whether it was just a trick to get information from the prisoner. Maximiano pushed João Estafeta aside.

"Let me question this animal," he said. "How about it, Bahian, how many soldiers have the Legalists got?"

The Bahian smiled slightly and shrugged his shoulders. The people waited in silence; they seemed to expect the prisoner to reveal something that would save the town from invasion.

"Speak, Bahian!" shouted Antoninho Bilheteiro. "If you don't we'll cut your tongue off before we drown you."

The Bahian said nothing. Antoninho Bilheteiro grabbed him, tore off the canvas bag, and bellowed:

"Talk, devil, and we'll let you live!"

Finally the Bahian spoke:

"I'm just sorry . . ." He paused a few seconds. "I'm just sorry that you had to do this shameful thing to me. Kill me? Of course you can kill me. But kill me with my clothes on, not with my private parts showing."

There was a murmur of astonishment among the people. A sudden impulse seized Antoninho Bilheteiro.

"Bahian!" he cried. "Before you die I must embrace you!"

The mulatto's hands were still tied, and the embrace would have made him fall if João Estafeta had not held him up.

At this moment Colonel Faria rode up on horseback. He had spent the day recruiting volunteers among the country people.

"What's going on here? Is this naked man our prisoner?"

Maximiano, bursting with enthusiasm, said:

"This mulatto is a real man even in the face of death!"

They told Colonel Faria what had happened. There was no need for the colonel to order the prisoner's hands to be untied, for João Estafeta had already untied them.

Antoninho Bilheteiro had a second generous impulse: he took

off his coat and put it on the Bahian. It came down only to his waist.

"Let's go," said Colonel Faria. "Come with me, Bahian. We'll go to my house and get some clothes for you."

The half-naked mulatto walked alongside the colonel's horse. The people formed a protective, moving circle so that any young ladies who might still be at the windows could not see him in this scandalous state.

Suddenly, from the distance, came the increasingly familiar yell:

"Allagwa gwa gwa! Allagwa gwa gwa!"

In Maximiano's store the Bahian was fortifying himself with a small glass of rum before returning to jail. Everyone gazed at him with admiration. From moment to moment, small boys came with presents sent by the families: tins of guava paste, cookies, tobacco. The prisoner awkwardly tried to express his thanks. When he smiled he revealed his white, pointed teeth, ferociously peaceful.

Every little while the wind brought the echo of a shot, the dim, persistent refrain of the civil war.

* * *

Rui Ribeiro Couto (1898–1963) was born in Santos, state of São Paulo, and died in Paris. A few years after his graduation from law school, he began a distinguished career in the diplomatic service.

In 1922 he participated in Modern Art Week, which initiated the dominance of modernism, but he stood out from most of his associates by the composure and restraint of his literary temperament. His poetry and fiction, chiefly short stories, earned him membership in the Brazilian Academy of Letters, to which he was elected in 1934.

"The Bahian" ("O Baiano") is from *Largo da Matriz e Outras Histórias,* 1940.

Dinah Silveira de Queiroz

Guidance

When people talk to me about virtue, about morality and im-
morality, about deportment, about anything, in short, that has to
do with right and wrong, I see Mama in my mind's eye. Not
exactly Mama. Just Mama's neck, her white, tremulous throat,
as she was enjoying one of her giggles. They sounded like someone delicately sipping coffee from a saucer. She used to laugh
this way chiefly at night when, with just the three of us in the
house, she would come to the dinner table in one of her gay,
loose, low-necked gowns as if she were going to a ball. She
would be so perfumed that the objects around her developed a
little atmosphere of their own and became lighter and more delicate. She never used rouge or lipstick, but she must have done
something to her skin to get that smoothness of freshly washed
china. On her, even perspiration was lovely, like moisture on
clear glass. Before such beauty, my face was a miserable and
busy topography, where I would explore furiously, and with
physical enjoyment, little underground caves in the deep, dark
pores, or tiny volcanoes which, to my pleasure, would burst between my nails. Mama's laugh was a "thank you so much" to my
father, who used to flatter her as if his life depended on her good
will. He tried, however, to conceal this adulation by joking and
by treating her eternally as a child. A long time before, a woman
spiritualist had said something to Mama that certainly must have
provoked her very best and special giggle:

"Why don't you try to exert a moral influence on people? You
don't realize it, but you have an extraordinary power over others.
You should go in for counseling. People sense your authority as
soon as they meet you. Give guidance. Your advice will never
fail. It comes from your mediumistic power . . ."

Mama repeated this four or five times among her lady friends and the idea caught on, in our town of Laterra.

If someone was contemplating a business transaction, you can be sure he'd show up at our house to get advice. On these occasions Mama, who was blonde and petite, seemed to grow taller and very erect, with her little head high and her chubby finger upraised. They used to consult Mama about politics and about marriages. Because everything she said was sensible and turned out to be correct, they began also to send wayward persons to her. Once a certain rich lady brought her son, an incorrigible drunkard. I remember that Mama said the most beautiful things about the reality of the Devil and about having to side with either the Beast or the Angel. She explained the misery in which the young man was foundering and scolded him with tremendous words. Her fat little finger was poised threateningly and her whole body trembled in righteous anger, although her voice was not raised above its natural tone. The young man and the lady wept together.

Papa was enchanted with the prestige which, as her husband, he enjoyed.

Quarrels between employer and employee, between husband and wife, between parents and children, all found their way to our house.

Mama would hear both sides, would advise, would moralize. And Papa, in his little shop, felt the influx of confidence spreading to his dominion.

It was at this time that Laterra found itself without a priest, for the vicar had died and the bishop had not yet sent a replacement. The townspeople had to go to Santo Antonio to get married or to baptize their children. But, for their novenas and their beads, they relied on my mother. Suddenly everyone became more religious. She would go to evening prayer in a lace veil, so fragrant and smooth of skin, so pure of face, that everybody said she looked like, and indeed was, a real saint. Untrue: a saint would not have emitted those little giggles, a saint would not have had so much fun. Fun is a sort of insult to the unhappy, and that is why Mama laughed and enjoyed herself only when we were alone.

One day, at the market fair in Laterra, a yokel asked:

"They say you got a lady priest here. Where does she live?"

Mama was told about it. She did not laugh.

"I don't like that." And she added: "I never was a religious fanatic. I'm just a normal person who wants to help her neighbor. If they go on with that kind of talk, I'll never take out my beads again."

But that very night, I saw her throat tremble with delight:

"Now they're calling me a lady priest. . . . Imagine!"

She had found her vocation. And she continued to give advice, to say fine things, to console those who lost their loved ones. Once, on the birthday of a man whose child she had god-mothered, Mama said such beautiful words about old age, about the flight of time, about the good we should do before night falls, that the man asked:

"Why don't you give a talk like this every Sunday? We have no vicar and the young people need guidance. . . ."

Everyone thought it an excellent idea. A society was founded, the Laterra Parents' Circle, which had its meetings at the city hall. People came from far away to hear Mama speak. Everybody said that she did an enormous amount of good to people's souls, that the sweetness of her words comforted those who were suffering. A number of individuals were converted by her. I think my father believed in her more than anyone else did. But I couldn't think of my mother as a predestined being, come to the world just to do good. It seemed to me that she was playacting and I felt a little ashamed. But at the same time I asked myself:

"Why should you feel this way? Doesn't she reconcile couples who have separated, doesn't she console widows, doesn't she even correct the incorrigible?"

One day, at lunchtime, Mama said to my father:

"Today they brought me a difficult case. . . . A strange young man. You're going to give him work. Just for the love of God. He came asking for help . . . and I must not turn him away. The poor boy cried so, he implored me . . . telling about his terrible problem. He's wretched!"

A dream of glory enticed her:

"Do you know that the doctors in Santo Antonio could do nothing for him? I want you to help me. I think it's important for him to work . . . here. It will cost you nothing. He says he wants to work for us free because he knows that I don't accept payment for my work either and do everything just out of kindness."

The new employee looked like a pretty girl. He was rosy-cheeked, had dark eyes with long lashes, moved about without making the least noise. He knew some poetry by heart and sometimes recited it in a soft voice while cleaning the counter in the store. When people learned that he was employed by us, they advised my father:

"This isn't the kind of person to work in a respectable house!"

"She wanted it," replied my father. "She always knows what she's doing."

The new employee worked with a will, but he had crises of anxiety. Although it was agreed that he would dine with us, on certain nights he did not do so. And he would appear later with his eyes red.

Many times, Mama shut herself in the living room with him and her quiet voice scolded and wounded him. She would also correct him before my father and even before me, but smiling with kindness:

"Take your hand away from your waist. You look like a girl, and if you act this way, then . . ."

But she knew how to say things that he surely wanted to hear:

"There is no one better than you on this earth! Why are you afraid of other people? Come on, lift up your head!"

Stimulated by this, my father guaranteed:

"In my house no one will ever insult you. I'd just like to see someone try!"

No one ever did. Even the boys in the street, who used to point at him and talk loudly and laugh, became serious and fled as soon as my father appeared at the door.

And for a long time the young man was never absent from dinner. In his leisure hours he made pretty things for Mama. He painted a fan for her and made a jar in the form of a swan, out of old, wet paper, glue, and heaven knows what. He became my friend. He knew about clothes and styles as nobody else did. He would express opinions about my dresses. At the hour of prayer he, who had been so humiliated, whose look had been that of a beaten creature, now would come and take a place next to Mama, with a chaplet in his hand. If visitors called while he was with us, he did not scurry away as he had previously done. He remained in a corner, looking at everyone calmly and amicably. I watched his gradual metamorphosis. Less timid, he had become less effeminate. His movements were more confident, his physical attitudes less ridiculous.

Mama, who had carefully watched her conversation when he was present, now virtually forgot that he was not one of us. She would laugh freely, with her delightful, tremulous giggles. She seemed to have stopped teaching him how to behave, for it was no longer necessary. And he, when not at the counter, began to follow her about. He helped her in the house, he went shopping with her. Mama had reproved certain young women for their love intrigues; seeing her pass by they would say, hidden behind their windows:

"Don't you think maybe she's cured him . . . too much?"

Laterra took pride in Mama, the most important person in the community. It pained many persons to observe that almost comical affection. They would see her walk by quickly, erect, with firm step, and the young man behind, carrying her packages, or at her side, holding her parasol with a certain fervor as if it had been a pallium in a religious procession. An obvious restlessness pervaded the city. It reached such a point that one Sunday, when Mama was talking on conjugal happiness and the duties of marriage, some heads turned toward the young man, almost imperceptibly but enough for me to perceive their thought. And an absurd feeling of expectation oppressed my heart.

Mama was the last to become aware of the passion she had aroused.

"Look," she said, "I only tried to build up his morale. . . . His own mother gave him up as lost—she even wished him dead! And today he's a fine young man! I'm only saying what everybody knows."

Papa was becoming despondent. One day he got it off his chest:

"I think it's better if he leaves. Obviously, you've succeeded in what you were trying to do. You've made him decent and hardworking, like anybody else. Let's thank God and send him back home. You did a wonderful job!"

"But," said Mama in amazement, "don't you see that more time is needed . . . so they'll forget about him? To send this boy back now would be a sin! A sin that I don't want on my conscience."

There was one night when the young man told a story at dinner about a hillbilly. Mama laughed as she had never laughed before, throwing back her petite head, showing her most disturbing nudity—her neck—with that tremulous chirp of hers. I saw his face become red and his eyes shine at the sight of her white splendor. Papa did not laugh. I felt happy and frightened. Three days later the young man fell ill with a grippe. It was while Mama was visiting him in his room that he said something to her. I'll never know what it was. For the first time, we heard Mama raise her voice. It was loud, strident, furious. A week later he was well and resumed work. She said to my father:

"You're right. It's time for him to go back home."

At dinner hour Mama told the maidservant:

"We'll be the only ones tonight. Just set three places . . ."

The next day, at the hour of prayer, the young man arrived in a state of fear, but he came along and took his usual place next to Mama.

"Go away!" she said in a low voice before beginning the prayer. He obeyed, not pleading even with his eyes.

Every head slowly followed him. I watched him, with his unobtrusive, schoolgirl walk, going out into the night.

In a few moments Mama's voice, slightly tremulous, was praying:

"Our Father who art in heaven, hallowed by Thy name. . . ."

The voices that accompanied hers were stronger than they had been in many days.

He did not return to his own town, where he had been the accepted object of ridicule. That very night a farmer, on leaving Laterra, saw a long shape swinging from a tree. He thought it might be an assailant, but he courageously approached the figure. He discovered the young man. We were called. I saw him. Mama didn't. By the light of the lantern he seemed more ridiculous than tragic . . . so frail, hanging there like a Judas with a face of purple cloth. An enormous crowd soon encircled the mango tree. I was convinced that all of Laterra was breathing easier. Now it had proof! Its lady had not transgressed, its moralist had not failed it.

For several months Mama, perfect and perfumed as always, uttered none of her giggles, although she continued, now without great conviction (I could tell), to give guidance. Even at dinner she wore dark dresses, closed at the neck.

* * *

DINAH SILVEIRA DE QUEIROZ was born in São Paulo in 1911. Her home is in Rio de Janeiro, but she has spent the greater part of the past few years in foreign countries with her husband, who is a diplomat.

Her first novel, published in 1939, was a great success and was made into a motion picture. On the basis of one of her later novels, she became the first woman writer to receive the Machado de Assis prize, the highest award granted by the Brazilian Academy of Letters. In addition to novels, she has written novellas, short stories, a children's book, and two plays. For many years she has done a daily newspaper column, which currently appears in the *Jornal do Comércio*.

"Guidance" ("A Moralista") was written in 1949. It is in the book *As Noites do Morro do Encanto,* 1957. Another of her stories was translated as "Sin" for *Mademoiselle,* August 1943.

Aurélio Buarque de Holanda

My Father's Hat

As early morning slowly invades the living room, the ashy light of the candles is sadder than ever. From my chair in the foyer I see father's hands crossed on his chest. His belly, like an inverted kettledrum, protrudes above the sides of the coffin. A stifled sob is heard. Some of the mourners have fallen asleep: a little truce with grief. My eyes burn, for I have wept much and slept little. My head rests upon the back of the easy chair, and for a moment I fool myself into thinking that I am calm and relaxed. I can see one of the windows from here; its black curtain moves gently, stirred by the morning breeze. On the rack in a corner of the foyer hangs a hat, like a thing abandoned. It is father's hat. It is a part of the man who lies there dead, his broad hands crossed on his chest, his face, in life so red, now a grayish white. It is something *of* him, something not destroyed by death.

My eyes stare at the hat. The brown, commonplace hat with bound brim, father's hat. The rack is chipped in the front, just as it always was when father used it. Although I try to curb my imagination, father begins to emerge, alive and stirring, from this object that was his. Looking at the hat from the side, I keep seeing his profile, the small but protrusive nose, the ruddy cheek (somewhat sunken in recent months), the short sideburn, the sparse, reddish-yellow mustache that he wore as long as I can remember.

The hat goes where father goes, casting a bit of shadow on his face. It is where it belongs, on father's head. Yes. There he is, returning home late in the afternoon, tired, already ailing. There he comes: the brown hat with brim turned down in front, that slow, slightly stooped way of walking that betokens old age. He puts his hat on the hat rack, right where I see it now, close to the mirror. He looks at himself in the mirror, rapidly strokes his mustache, and goes on into the dining room, where he sits down and begins to talk with mother about endless day-to-day things. Mother tells him what happened at home: the water was shut off, the milk was sour, she had trouble with the maid:

"I never heard such impertinence!"

Father complains about business conditions, which are going from bad to worse:

"It's terrible. Trade is practically at a standstill, and all the government thinks of is taxes and more taxes. I don't know where it will end."

But mother is calm:

"Don't worry so. We'll get along. The boys are working, they'll help out. Be patient."

He will say that he's worked all his life in the hope that he and she would have an untroubled old age.

The hat remains there on the rack until the next day, for during the past few months father has rarely gone out at night. Anyone looking at the hat rack knows for certain that the master of the house is at home. Not merely by a process of reasoning based on the presence of the hat, but because in looking at the hat he can see father. One might almost point to the hat and say, "Look at Manuel there."

The next morning father puts on his hat with great care. He examines himself slowly in the mirror. He is closely shaven. He always used a straight-edge razor, never a safety razor. He finally gives his approval to what he sees. His face is somewhat drawn; there are crow's feet near the eyes (he draws the skin taut with his fingers); deep lines extend from his nostrils to the corners of his mouth. . . . But he gives his approval. Only one thing is seriously wrong: several of his teeth are missing. He ought to get upper and lower dental plates. But no, that would be foolish. He's not going to go around grinning all the time, and when his mouth is closed, the gaps don't affect his facial expression. His complexion is good; his wavy blond hair shows only a few silver threads despite his sixty-odd years; there are no signs of baldness; and his eyes, like those of his Portuguese grandfather, are light blue behind his elegant gold-rimmed glasses.

"Manuel!"

"What is it?" he says, a little annoyed for he is adjusting the break in his hat. "All right, I'll bring it, don't worry."

He has the hat looking exactly right now.

He goes out. He doffs his hat, poising it just above his head, as he greets a neighbor: "Good morning, Dona Hortensia." The neighbor melts into a smile. (Mother doesn't like these smiles of Dona Hortensia.) Every few moments father lifts his hat, for he knows everybody on our street. Sometimes the greeting is less formal, just a touch of his fingers on the brim. And down the street goes father with his hat, an essential complement of his head and virtually an organic part of the man.

If, upon arriving at his store, he finds anything out of order, his hat may, for a few moments, lose its customary dignity and composure. Father may beat it in rage against the counter as if hitting someone. But once his anger ends, he will begin to re-compose his hat in proper shape. He will smooth it out, make a furrow in it, and, with the tips of his fingers, make the sides just a little concave. Done.

During lunch hour all places of business are closed, and there are few people in the streets. Father is hungry, so he puts on his hat less carefully and walks less slowly than at other times. If it is a warm day he will arrive home in a sweat, wiping his face with his handkerchief.

"Jesus, what heat! Nobody can take this kind of weather."

He will bathe before lunch and will talk, as usual, about the terrible slump in business.

The baker's man leaves the bread at the door. People start to pass by—humble people who begin their work while the cocks are still crowing, so that they may survive and may guaranty the prosperity of the more fortunate. Someone inside is weeping convulsively; it is my sister.

The hat hangs there on the rack, an abandoned, useless relic of a fallen warrior. Using it as a point of reference, I start to reconstitute an entire past, although not in chronological sequence. The weeping brings me back to the reality of the moment, and now the hat offers me a very recent image of father. He entered the hospital, wearing his inseparable hat, and took it off, never indeed to put it on again. He was very pale. He writhed with pain. Then suddenly the hat went back on father's head, and he walked along, doffing it occasionally to greet someone or to show respect as a funeral procession went by or as he passed a church. And when I brought his hat back from the hospital five or six hours ago, it seemed to me that I was carrying a bit—no, an essential part—of my father. He, or the rest of him, remained on the death bed until he was brought home in an automobile and placed there in the coffin in the parlor, with his pale face, his swollen belly, and his hands crossed upon his chest.

The candles have almost burned out. The wax drips down and accumulates at the bottom of the candlesticks. Behind the head of the coffin stands a crucifix—a metal Christ for whose consoling presence Mr. Sampaio, the mortician, charges high, explaining that it is not a question of rental, for "holiness can be neither bought nor hired."

Father used to talk to me about the Holy Trinity, which I had some difficulty in understanding. He believed in God, in religion. He did not hold with priests, however, and even when he knew his death was imminent he did not seek a confessor. He was a Catholic, but he did not share the aversion that some felt for Protestants and he occasionally attended a session of the Spiritists. This religious eclecticism did not interfere with his powerful, deeply ingrained faith in God, which never deserted him, even in his last moments. When he made plans for the future, God invariably came into the picture as the Power on which the realization of the plans depended:

"This year things went very badly. But next year, if business improves, with God's help I'll . . ."

If he was wearing his hat he would take it off and would raise it for a moment, very respectfully, as he said "with God's help." "I have faith in God," "God will come to my aid," "God is my father"—he never spoke these things without removing his hat.

I turn to a picture of him as a young man in the early days of the Republic. It is so faded that one can barely distinguish his features. He was still living in Tatuamunha, his place of birth. He often talked about the *pastoris*—musical folk plays—as they were given in those days (those grand old days!), of the charm of some of the girls who played the shepherdesses, of the delightful songs they sang, and of the passion they aroused in all the young men of his circle. I can imagine my father enchanted by the beauty of one of these country girls, for he was young, ardent, romantic, and even liked poetry a little. The shepherdesses in their two groups, the Red Cordon and the Blue Cordon, danced merrily onto the stage shaking their tambourines.

> "Gracious friends, to Bethlehem
>   Come with this shepherdess
> To see the blessed Baby born
>   For our happiness."

Other numbers followed. The fellow who played the shepherd was always dragging his crook. At one point Old Fury leaped onto the stage and shouted:

> "Oh, I am a spirit malign.
> I ask you to be mine,
>   But whether you will or nay
>   I'll carry you away."

The shepherdesses sang again and again. The people in the audience divided themselves now into two groups, each favoring one of the cordons. Father was on the side of the Blue Cordon. There were arguments. The girl who played the Contramestra (chief shepherdess of the Blue Cordon) was marvelous. She swayed so gracefully, sang so beautifully, and gave father such a warm, sententious look, that he felt that old Lusitanian sensuality surging through his veins.

"Bravo, Contramestra!"

"Hurrah, Mestra!"

The opposing factions almost came to blows. There were presents, lots of presents. One enthusiast gave something to the Mestra and to every member of the Red Cordon. More songs by each cordon. Then Diana sang:

> "I am Diana, I choose no side,
>   I applaud them both with zest.
> But, gentle people, what say you?
>   Which cordon sings the best?"

A few of the fans insisted that Diana join one of the cordons: "Diana, come on over to the Red!"

"No, Diana, the Blue, the Blue!"

Indeed, Diana profited from her neutrality, receiving gifts from both sides.

Some of the partisans had had a little to drink. They became more and more ecstatic. Some threw their hats in the air and then threw them on the stage.

"Step on my hat, Mestra!"

More applause.

"Bravo for the Blue Cordon!"

The Contramestra came forward and held out a carnation to my father:

> "Oh Manuel,
>   Be kind to me:
> Accept this flower
> I offer thee."

Father swaggered up the steps to the stage, put the flower in his buttonhole, and placed a crackling new banknote in the neck of the Contramestra's dress. The partisans of the Blue Cordon applauded deliriously.

Father came down again, in a state of glory. The performance lasted till dawn, by which time father's hat would doubtless have flown through the air for the Contramestra to step on.

What kind of hat did he wear in those days? Was it black and solemn, with the brim turned up at the sides? Was it a straw hat? No matter. For me, the hat hanging there on the rack is the hat that father must always have worn. It is father's hat. There it goes, up in the air, and falls on the stage, where the shepherd-esses are singing. Kerosene lamps, hung on rickety wooden posts, light up not only the stage but the entire square in front of the Church of Saint Gonçalo. (How plaintive were the voices in the church when they sang the novena: "Saint Gonçalo de Amarante, our glorious patron . . . !" Feminine voices, warm with faith, asking their saint for happiness, good fishing for their husbands, good crops in the fields and destruction to the ants who were invading them, good marriages for their daughters, the cure of their sons stricken with malaria. They prayed for peace and plenty for their humble homes, dwarfed by the palm trees that shaded almost the entire village.) Near the venders' trays additional illumination is furnished by torches of castor seeds strung on long stalks. The crowd presses around the various attractions. It is a lively festival.

Many gather in front of the auction platform. The auctioneer's words come loud, slow, and clear:

"I hear a thousand reis for this fine watermelon presented to Saint Gonçalo, worker of miracles."

Someone offers five hundred more.

"I hear fifteen hundred."

"Two thousand reis."

They all want to own the saint's watermelon. Before long they are bidding five thousand.

"Six thousand reis to keep Silva's hands off it."

"Six thousand reis," repeats the auctioneer.

"Sixty-five hundred to keep Chico from smelling it."

Finally, when no one offers more, the auctioneer declares:

"I'll hold the bidding ended if now I hear no higher. I give you once, I give you twice, I give you thrice. Sold and delivered."

A big attraction now is the naval folk play. At the top of a mast the lookout, obeying orders, scans the horizon to see if he can descry "the land of Spain and the strand of Portugal." He sings, and in his nasal drawl, as in the voices of the rest of the crew of the good ship *Catarineta,* there is a touch of melancholy.

Indifferent to the auction, uninterested in the naval pageant, father is wholly engrossed in the pastoral play. He cleans his crushed and dusty hat while the shepherdesses amaze the audience with their singing and the partisans sweat with ecstasy.

Firecrackers burst in the air. Father takes off his hat and uses it to protect his face from the flying fragments.

A few years go by. Mother, summering with some relatives in town, is glad to get away from the monotony of the sugar plantation. Father is serenading her under a moon so bright that it almost turns the evening into day. The courtship has begun. Some days earlier he passed through the portal of her house with an acacia blossom in his lapel (meaning: "I dreamed about you"), and the young lady gave him a smile that made his head swim. Mama's uncle also is in love with her and, for a while, provides competition. But father puts into his voice that old Portuguese yearning and, with his hat carelessly tilted back over the nape of his neck, sings to his love:

> "O pallor pure, o pallor blest,
>   O pallor of thy tranquil face,
> It has deprived me of my rest,
>   It is my scourge and my disgrace."

His voice is deep until "deprived." Then it rises to a prolonged high note on "scourge." It falls again, after a little cadenza into which father puts his whole heart, doubtless depriving his loved one of *her* rest.

What was the first thing he did on his trip to Maceió, made shortly before he proposed to her? He bought the *Dictionary of Roots, Flowers, Leaves, and Fruits,* so that he could tell his loved one, to whom he had never spoken, what his eyes and hands could not express. I can imagine the embarrassment of the country boy as he entered the bookstore, holding his hat in his hands and twisting its brim, almost unwilling to ask for the book lest he expose the purity of his feeling to strangers who might sully it.

One day, after they become engaged, he rides out to the Good Hope Plantation, proud on his nut-brown horse. He alights, takes off his hat, and, very respectfully, greets his fiancée and Dona Luisa, his future mother-in-law. They converse for a time in the enormous parlor, whose walls are covered with family pictures, while Maria Araquã, a former slave, lights the elaborate kerosene lamp hung from the ceiling. Later they go to the dining room. Dona Luisa always sits at the head of the long patriarchal table. Father sits down at her right, directly facing his loved one. For him, it is as if his future brothers-in-law and sisters-in-law did not exist. He is so very self-important, with his wavy blond hair parted on the left and his mustache fairly begging him to stroke it. He handles the silverware with aristocratic delicacy, but eats very little. "You're not enjoying your meal," says Dona Luisa. He replies that everything is excellent. However, he refuses, with a sophisticated smile, most of the dishes offered him. After dinner, grandmother orders the tablecloth removed, and father reads aloud the first chapter of a novel by

Escrich which he and his future mother-in-law greatly relish. From time to time his eyes seek those, modestly lowered, of his sweetheart. He reads beautifully, with unhurried emphasis, bringing out the meaning of each passage and adopting inflections suitable to the speech of each of the characters. The dialogue comes animated and alive from his lips. It is a pleasure to listen to him.

The next day, on the porch, he says goodbye to everyone and gallops off on his horse, waving his hat to them just before he disappears around the bend.

How haughty, almost cocky, is father's hat on his wedding day! Our cavalier is wearing a dark suit, Bostock high-laced shoes, a white shirt with stiff, gleaming front, collar, and cuffs—and a black hat with high crown and curved brim. How elegantly he removes it as he comes in and receives the first congratulations. A little later, affected by the emotional excitement, father feels very warm and uses his hat as a fan.

The sun rises. Traffic in the street increases. Passers-by pause at the open door and look at the coffin. The maidservant comes in, is shocked to see the corpse, and begins to cry. Coffee is being prepared. Sounds of various sorts fill the house. Mother is sobbing loudly. She calls me. As I get up I look at the corpse, stiff, ashy pale, hands crossed upon the chest, belly swollen. Father is wearing an old cutaway coat, dating from I don't know when. The burial will be at ten.

The black curtains are fluttering. The wind, now strong, invades the house and makes the light of the candles dance in an agony of indecision. Walking toward mother, I see father's hat on the rack near the mirror. It sways in the wind—abandoned, sad, forgotten—as if it were waving, calling for someone . . .

* * *

Aurélio Buarque de Holanda Ferreira was born in 1910 in Passo de Camaragibe, Alagoas. He showed a scholarly bent at an early age, with special proficiency in languages, and began to teach when only sixteen years old. He took a law degree and held several municipal offices, including that of director of the Municipal Library, in the state capital, Maceió. In 1938 he moved to Rio de Janeiro, where he has engaged in various literary and pedagogical activities. In 1961 he was elected to membership in the Brazilian Academy of Letters.

Apart from his eminence as a writer of short stories, Buarque de Holanda has distinguished himself as a philologist, anthologist, literary essayist, translator, and editor. Brazil's foremost lexicographer, he is currently preparing a multi-volume *Grande Dicionário Brasileiro da Língua Portuguêsa.*

"My Father's Hat" ("O Chapéu de Meu Pai") is from *Dois Mundos,* 1942.

Marília São Paulo Penna e Costa

The Happiest Couple in the World

"Why do you always write about such wretched marriages? Just once, I wish you'd tell a story about a happy couple."

The young lady who hurled this challenge at me the other day is intelligent and pretty. One can see love fairly leaping from her face. Moreover, she has been married two years and is still supremely cheerful about it. I should not like to contribute in any way to a change in her disposition, nor do I wish to provoke others, similarly minded, to charge me with cynicism or morbidity. . . . Accordingly, I shall write about the happiest couple I ever knew. I have always tried, in my stories, to represent problems at once common and profoundly human. This time, to please my young critic, I shall have to take a wholly different tack.

I met them in 1949. After three days of sightseeing and shopping in Brussels, I had decided to take in Bruges, the city of lace and beautiful monuments, where, in the cold silence of the churches, the Gothic permeates everything.

I visited the cathedral. Then, as it was raining, I dropped into a store, where a hobbling, bespectacled little old lady sold articles of lace made by the orphan girls at a local charity school. I bought some tablecloths and waited for the rain to let up. When it did, I started across a bridge toward my car, parked on the other side. An elderly couple was crossing at the same time, and I felt a sudden joy at hearing them speak Portuguese, an unmistakably Brazilian Portuguese:

"What a downpour that was! We've been having terrible weather. . . ."

I approached them and introduced myself as a compatriot— the best possible credential in a foreign country. I invited them to have coffee with me in a little café nearby. They accepted.

They soon informed me that he was from Rio, she was from Espírito Santo, and they had been married fifty years. Not very surprisingly, it was the lady, Dona Eulina, who did most of the talking. Her voice was strong, and both the tone and content of her words made it abundantly evident that she liked to travel, to see the world; also, that she adored her husband, who, quite obviously, was the one and only love of her life.

We exchanged remarks about hotels, stores, restaurants. Then Dona Eulina explained why they were in Bruges. Dr. Cândido poured himself some coffee and let a little of the cream, thick and fatty, drip into the yellow cup. The attentiveness with which he listened to his wife manifested eloquently his esteem and admiration. Behind his glasses, his small, shining eyes fairly caressed her.

"It was I," she said, "who insisted on coming back to Bruges, because I liked it best of all the places we visited on our honeymoon. Such a long time ago . . . fifty years. I didn't want to have a big party or a public mass in Rio. There was no reason for anything like that. We have no one left. We preferred to take a trip to Europe. We hadn't been abroad since before the war. . . . We picked the exact date of our marriage to be here in Bruges again. They were so wonderful, those days we spent here. . . . We ordered a special mass for today in the cathedral. It was an act of thanksgiving. Just for us two, nobody else. We confessed and took communion, just as we always do on this day. Cândido wanted a mass with music. It couldn't have been more wonderful. Five violins, two organs. And all the lights on. There are no flowers here this time of year, so Cândido chartered an airplane to bring some up from the Riviera. The tremendous, empty nave, all lit and decorated like a fairyland. The soft music of Liszt's *Rêve d'amour,* so appropriate to us. No one else there, and Cândido and I so full of happiness we didn't even notice we were alone."

"Have you any children?" I asked.

Dr. Cândido blinked as his wife quickly replied:

"No, and we never felt the need of them. Cândido and I are not just husband and wife, we are inseparable friends. In fifty years of marriage Cândido has never eaten breakfast alone. I get up with him every day; ever since the beginning, when he still practiced medicine. He's retired now and we have enough to live comfortably the rest of our lives."

"Have you no close relatives?"

"We have a raft of nephews and nieces. Our brothers and sisters and our in-laws have all passed on. I was the youngest in my family, and Cândido was in his."

They told me their itinerary. They planned to go to Paris, to the Côte d'Azur, and then back to Brazil by ship. They were afraid of airplanes.

"Why don't you visit the United States before you go home?"

"We'll go there some day. But pretty soon we'll be getting homesick for our little corner of the world. Long trips are only for young people—although generally it's the old ones who can afford them. We mainly wanted to see Bruges again, to celebrate our golden wedding here. It's today, you know."

We toasted the occasion with their favorite liqueur. They were smiling at each other. I was an intruder in that world of memories. We exchanged cards with a vague promise to meet again back in Rio.

Some months later I got in touch with them. They were most hospitable, and I visited them several times at the house on Alice Street where they had lived ever since their marriage. I noticed her tendency to make continual little demands of him, with which he always complied graciously.

On one occasion they showed me an album of photographs. There she was, a pretty bride, smiling with the air of a woman who had made up her mind to be happy. Behind prodigiously large mustaches, her groom seemed to be hiding a timid acquiescence to whatever the world had in store for him. On subsequent pages there were snapshots of them in Europe, sitting in an automobile or strolling in the Bois de Boulogne. One picture showed them in the public gardens in Bruges, holding hands and posing stiffly for the street photographer.

"We had to sit there for twenty minutes without moving a muscle to produce this horror," remarked Dona Eulina.

As she spoke, Dr. Cândido took a picture of a baby, which was loose in the album, and quickly, almost surreptitiously, placed it between two pages that we had already seen. She gave no sign of having noticed this and continued to show me pictures and documents illustrating their now fifty-two years of happy married life.

Then she served tea. Everything was so right, so perfectly organized, that the home of these dear old people seemed almost an earthly paradise. Their hobby was gardening. Dr. Cândido took care of the bromelias, and Dona Eulina spent part of every day with her roses. They also loved songbirds. In particular they collected Belgian canaries, which on sunny mornings provided joyful background music to the life of this inseparable couple.

I remember the last time I was there. It was in 1956. They were about to start on another trip to Europe, where they would of course visit Bruges and from which they planned to go to the United States. It was hard to believe that such vigor, such love, and such eagerness could survive fifty-seven years of marriage.

I wished them everything good, if indeed there was room for any more happiness in their lives.

"I think I'm the luckiest woman in the world," replied Dona Eulina. "I doubt if there ever was another couple that went through fifty-seven years of married life without one single argument."

"That's right," said her husband, "not one."

"So what more can we possibly desire? Except to go on like this to our diamond wedding anniversary—which isn't so far off."

"The only thing we might pray for, if we have the right to ask for anything more, is that when one of us dies the other will die too and not have to live on alone."

I said goodbye, adding that I would see them on their return.

They sent me a postcard from Bruges: "Do you remember our golden wedding anniversary here? Hope you won't forget these two old dotards who just can't fall out of love. Eulina and Cândido."

From Belgium they went to Italy, visiting several cities there, and in Genoa they took the *Andrea Doria* for their first trip to the United States. With dismay I read that they were among the missing when the ship collided, in the silence of the night, with a Swedish freighter.

They died together, just as they had wished. They had fulfilled their mission of tenderness, love, and happiness—words which, however often repeated, never become tiresome.

While strolling along Alice Street with a friend, I saw that the old house was being torn down, doubtless to make way for the construction of a modern apartment building. I told my companion, a lady in late middle age, the beautiful story of the couple who had died together at sea after fifty-seven years of perfect marriage. She listened with great interest.

A few days later my friend telephoned to tell me that she had found out something curious about Eulina and her husband. It seemed that Dr. Cândido had come home one day carrying a newborn baby boy. He had been called suddenly by an acquaintance to perform the delivery and could not refuse. The mother was penniless.

Dona Eulina raised the child with loving care, until she noticed its facial resemblance to her husband. As the boy grew older the resemblance grew stronger. She began to hate the child. She scolded it for the slightest transgression. Sometimes, when her husband was out, she beat the little boy. Finally she elicited a complete confession from Cândido. Then she became a monster of evil. She screamed at her husband. She cursed him repeatedly and ordered him to take the child and get out. He kneeled and begged forgiveness. He told her that she could be sure he would have nothing more to do with the woman, for indeed she had died in childbirth. Dona Eulina screamed again and struck him in the face with the heel of her slipper, saying that if the woman had been alive he would still have been deceiving her. Dr. Cândido begged her to have pity for the child, who bore no share in his guilt. He prostrated himself: he became her doormat.

One night, in an access of rage, she went out and placed the child, then three years old, in the turnbox of an orphanage. She told her husband that the boy had run away and that he could go look for him if he wished.

A woman informed Dr. Cândido that she had seen Dona Eulina go out with the child wrapped in a blanket. He went everywhere looking for his son, but it never occurred to him that the boy might be in the orphanage. Finally, after many desperate days and sleepless nights, he gave up.

I did not believe this story. All the people on Alice Street considered them a model couple. They had lived in the same house for fifty-seven years. If Dona Eulina had been a virago, her neighbors would certainly have known about it.

At the mass (it had been announced in the papers) commemorating the first anniversary of their death, I found a half-dozen dry-eyed ladies mechanically counting their beads and muttering a meaningless prayer. I inquired, hoping to find one of the numerous nieces and nephews that Dona Eulina had mentioned. A thin, pious-looking old lady, with warts on her face, pointed to a woman with grayish hair kneeling at a side altar.

"That's her daughter."

As I must have looked astonished, the outspoken old lady added with a certain maliciousness:

"You mean you didn't know she had a child?"

Curving her wrinkled hand and placing it at the side of her mouth, the old lady whispered in my ear:

"She had it by another man. He knew all about it and arranged for the girl to be brought up in a charity home. He knew he couldn't have children. . . . The girl grew up without ever meeting them, but they saw that she got everything she needed."

The old lady chuckled with scornful glee. I walked past the kneeling woman and sought some resemblance to Dona Eulina. There was none. She looked too old to be Dona Eulina's child. She seemed insecure, downcast, beaten, in contrast to her always triumphant mother. The altar at which she was praying was not the altar used in the mass. But why would the warted old lady lie to a total stranger?

"You mean her mother is Dona Eulina, wife of Dr. Cândido?"

"Of course! You think I'd say it if it wasn't true? I've known about this child since she was born. She looks old because she's had a miserable life. She found out who she was. Her mother would never see her. Cândido forbade it."

I left in a state of emotional bewilderment. Perhaps the old lady was senile. But I remembered, that day in Bruges when I asked whether they had any children, how quickly she answered that they did not, while a spark in Dr. Cândido's eyes seemed to contradict her. I remembered also the picture of a baby between pages of the album.

I became intrigued. I talked with several of the neighbors, but they could tell me nothing of a child, for they were all of a later generation. I considered it unlikely that I could get any pertinent information from the nephews and nieces; I had learned, through a friend of a friend of a grandniece, that the couple had quarreled with their relatives more than half a century before. Mutual hatred had kept them apart ever after. The new generation did not even know Dona Eulina and Dr. Cândido.

The grandniece explained the matter to my friend's friend:

"Grandma said they were a couple of nuts and that they had no friends at all. They lived almost like hermits ever since a child that they adopted died of yellow fever. Nobody ever saw the body. They said they were going to send it to a cemetery in Belgium. There was no funeral or anything, and they wouldn't talk about the child to anyone, not even to each other."

This story seemed to me to make sense, until a week later when I talked with a doctor, a very old man, and asked him whether he had been acquainted with Dr. Cândido.

"I know him," he replied. "That is, I knew him. They died in the wreck of the *Andrea Doria*. A strange case of reciprocal neurosis. If I hadn't witnessed it myself, if I had read about it somewhere, I might not have believed it. They had a pathological need to think of themselves as one-hundred-percent happy. And for a time they almost seemed to be. Then they had a child, which you might think would have made their lives complete. But she began to complain that the child had spoiled things for them, that it cried and was a nuisance and robbed them of the peace of mind they needed for their eternal love. He finally caught this attitude from her. They hired someone to take care of the boy. When he was a little older, they sent him to a boarding school in Bruges, in Belgium.

"They paid for everything he needed. But they never wanted to see him again. Before long, it seems, the boy died of pneumonia. They weren't the least disturbed. They continued to adore each other and to shut out all consciousness of sin or misery. They were, you might say, insanely happy."

* * *

MARÍLIA SÃO PAULO PENNA E COSTA, the youngest of the authors represented in this collection, was born in 1930 in Rio de Janeiro, where she still lives (in Copacabana). She has written for many newspapers; she is an inveterate world traveler, and her contributions at present are chiefly on travel and tourism. Mrs. Penna e Costa has produced three novels, the most recent of which, published in 1966, gained first place in the Brazilian best-seller list.

"The Happiest Couple in the World" ("O Casal Mais Feliz do Mundo") is from her only book of short stories, *Mãos Grisalhas,* 1962.

João Guimarães Rosa

The Third Bank of the River

My father was a dutiful, orderly, straightforward man. And according to several reliable people of whom I inquired, he had had these qualities since adolescence or even childhood. By my own recollection, he was neither jollier nor more melancholy than the other men we knew. Maybe a little quieter. It was mother, not father, who ruled the house. She scolded us daily— my sister, my brother, and me. But it happened one day that father ordered a boat.

He was very serious about it. It was to be made specially for him, of mimosa wood. It was to be sturdy enough to last twenty or thirty years and just large enough for one person. Mother carried on plenty about it. Was her husband going to become a fisherman all of a sudden? Or a hunter? Father said nothing. Our house was less than a mile from the river, which around there was deep, quiet, and so wide you couldn't see across it.

I can never forget the day the rowboat was delivered. Father showed no joy or other emotion. He just put on his hat as he always did and said goodbye to us. He took along no food or bundle of any sort. We expected mother to rant and rave, but she didn't. She looked very pale and bit her lip, but all she said was:

"If you go away, stay away. Don't ever come back!"

Father made no reply. He looked gently at me and motioned me to walk along with him. I feared mother's wrath, yet I eagerly obeyed. We headed toward the river together. I felt bold and exhilarated, so much so that I said:

"Father, will you take me with you in your boat?"

He just looked at me, gave me his blessing, and, by a gesture, told me to go back. I made as if to do so but, when his back was turned, I ducked behind some bushes to watch him. Father got into the boat and rowed away. Its shadow slid across the water like a crocodile, long and quiet.

Father did not come back. Nor did he go anywhere, really. He just rowed and floated across and around, out there in the river. Everyone was appalled. What had never happened, what could not possibly happen, was happening. Our relatives, neighbors, and friends came over to discuss the phenomenon.

Mother was ashamed. She said little and conducted herself with great composure. As a consequence, almost everyone thought (though no one said it) that father had gone insane. A few, however, suggested that father might be fulfilling a promise he had made to God or to a saint, or that he might have some horrible disease, maybe leprosy, and that he left for the sake of the family, at the same time wishing to remain fairly near them.

Travelers along the river and people living near the bank on one side or the other reported that father never put foot on land, by day or night. He just moved about on the river, solitary, aimless, like a derelict. Mother and our relatives agreed that the food which he had doubtless hidden in the boat would soon give out and that then he would either leave the river and travel off somewhere (which would be at least a little more respectable) or he would repent and come home.

How far from the truth they were! Father had a secret source of provisions: me. Every day I stole food and brought it to him. The first night after he left, we all lit fires on the shore and prayed and called to him. I was deeply distressed and felt a need to do something more. The following day I went down to the river with a loaf of corn bread, a bunch of bananas, and some bricks of raw brown sugar. I waited impatiently a long, long hour. Then I saw the boat, far off, alone, gliding almost imperceptibly on the smoothness of the river. Father was sitting in the bottom of the boat. He saw me but he did not row toward me or make any gesture. I showed him the food and then I placed it in a hollow rock on the river bank; it was safe there from animals, rain, and dew. I did this day after day, on and on and on. Later I learned, to my surprise, that mother knew what I was doing and left food around where I could easily steal it. She had a lot of feelings she didn't show.

Mother sent for her brother to come and help on the farm and in business matters. She had the schoolteacher come and tutor us children at home because of the time we had lost. One day, at her request, the priest put on his vestments, went down to the shore, and tried to exorcise the devils that had got into my father. He shouted that father had a duty to cease his unholy obstinacy. Another day she arranged to have two soldiers come and try to frighten him. All to no avail. My father went by in the distance, sometimes so far away he could barely be seen. He never replied to anyone and no one ever got close to him. When some newspapermen came in a launch to take his picture, father headed his boat to the other side of the river and into the marshes, which he knew like the palm of his hand but in which other people quickly got lost. There in his private maze, which extended for miles, with heavy foliage overhead and rushes on all sides, he was safe.

We had to get accustomed to the idea of father's being out on the river. We had to but we couldn't, we never could. I think I was the only one who understood to some degree what our father wanted and what he did not want. The thing I could not understand at all was how he stood the hardship. Day and night, in sun and rain, in heat and in the terrible midyear cold spells, with his old hat on his head and very little other clothing, week after week, month after month, year after year, unheedful of the waste and emptiness in which his life was slipping by. He never set foot on earth or grass, on isle or mainland shore. No doubt he sometimes tied up the boat at a secret place, perhaps at the tip of some island, to get a little sleep. He never lit a fire or even struck a match and he had no flashlight. He took only a small part of the food that I left in the hollow rock—not enough, it seemed to me, for survival. What could his state of health have been? How about the continual drain on his energy, pulling and pushing the oars to control the boat? And how did he survive the anual floods, when the river rose and swept along with it all sorts of dangerous objects—branches of trees, dead bodies of animals—that might suddenly crash against his little boat?

He never talked to a living soul. And we never talked about him. We just thought. No, we could never put our father out of mind. If for a short time we seemed to, it was just a lull from which we would be sharply awakened by the realization of his frightening situation.

My sister got married, but mother didn't want a wedding party. It would have been a sad affair, for we thought of him every time we ate some especially tasty food. Just as we thought of him in our cozy beds on a cold, stormy night—out there, alone and unprotected, trying to bail out the boat with only his hands and a gourd. Now and then someone would say that I was getting to look more and more like my father. But I knew that by then his hair and beard must have been shaggy and his nails long. I pictured him thin and sickly, black with hair and sunburn, and almost naked despite the articles of clothing I occasionally left for him.

He didn't seem to care about us at all. But I felt affection and respect for him, and, whenever they praised me because I had done something good, I said:

"My father taught me to act that way."

It wasn't exactly accurate but it was a truthful sort of lie. As I said, father didn't seem to care about us. But then why did he stay around there? Why didn't he go up the river or down the river, beyond the possibility of seeing us or being seen by us? He alone knew the answer.

My sister had a baby boy. She insisted on showing father his grandson. One beautiful day we all went down to the river bank, my sister in her white wedding dress, and she lifted the baby high. Her husband held a parasol above them. We shouted to father and waited. He did not appear. My sister cried; we all cried in each other's arms.

My sister and her husband moved far away. My brother went to live in a city. Times changed, with their usual imperceptible rapidity. Mother finally moved too; she was old and went to live with her daughter. I remained behind, a leftover. I could never think of marrying. I just stayed there with the impedimenta of of my life. Father, wandering alone and forlorn on the river, needed me. I knew he needed me, although he never even told me why he was doing it. When I put the question to people bluntly and insistently, all they told me was that they heard that father had explained it to the man who made the boat. But now this man was dead and nobody knew or remembered anything. There was just some foolish talk, when the rains were especially severe and persistent, that my father was wise like Noah and had the boat built in anticipation of a new flood; I dimly remember people saying this. In any case, I would not condemn my father for what he was doing. My hair was beginning to turn gray.

I have only sad things to say. What bad had I done, what was my great guilt? My father always away and his absence always with me. And the river, always the river, perpetually renewing itself. The river, always. I was beginning to suffer from old age, in which life is just a sort of lingering. I had attacks of illness and of anxiety. I had a nagging rheumatism. And he? Why, why was he doing it? He must have been suffering terribly. He was so old. One day, in his failing strength, he might let the boat capsize; or he might let the current carry it downstream, on and on, until it plunged over the waterfall to the boiling turmoil below. It pressed upon my heart. He was out there and I was forever robbed of my peace. I am guilty of I know not what, and my pain is an open wound inside me. Perhaps I would know— if things were different. I began to guess what was wrong.

Out with it! Had I gone crazy? No, in our house that word was never spoken, never through all the years. No one called anybody crazy, for nobody is crazy. Or maybe everybody. All I did was go there and wave a handkerchief. So he would be more likely to see me. I was in complete command of myself. I waited. Finally he appeared in the distance, there, then over there, a vague shape sitting in the back of the boat. I called to him several times. And I said what I was so eager to say, to state formally and under oath. I said it as loud as I could:

"Father, you have been out there long enough. You are old. . . . Come back, you don't have to do it anymore. . . . Come back and I'll go instead. Right now, if you want. Any time. I'll get into the boat. I'll take your place."

And when I had said this my heart beat more firmly.

He heard me. He stood up. He maneuvered with his oars and headed the boat toward me. He had accepted my offer. And suddenly I trembled, down deep. For he had raised his arm and waved—the first time in so many, so many years. And I couldn't . . . In terror, my hair on end, I ran, I fled madly. For he seemed to come from another world. And I'm begging forgiveness, begging, begging.

I experienced the dreadful sense of cold that comes from deadly fear, and I became ill. Nobody ever saw or heard about him again. Am I a man, after such a failure? I am what never should have been. I am what must be silent. I know it is too late. I must stay in the deserts and unmarked plains of my life, and I fear I shall shorten it. But when death comes I want them to take me and put me in a little boat in this perpetual water between the long shores; and I, down the river, lost in the river, inside the river . . . the river . . .

* * *

JOÃO GUIMARÃES ROSA was born in 1908 in Cordisburgo, Minas Gerais. He practiced medicine for several years, part of the time in the backlands of Minas. In 1934 he began a diplomatic career, which carried him to Germany, France, and other countries. He has held the rank of ambassador since 1958. Still with the Ministry of Foreign Affairs, he now occupies an important post in Rio de Janeiro.

Apart from an unpublished volume of verse, his first book was a collection of short stories, *Sagarana,* published in 1946. This book and his only full-length novel, *The Devil to Pay in the Backlands,* have been published in English translation. Guimarães Rosa has also produced a collection of novellas and another book of short stories, *Primeiras Estórias,* 1962, from which "The Third Bank of the River" ("A Terceira Margem do Rio") is taken.

Many Brazilians consider Guimarães Rosa their most important contemporary writer. He is noted for the unconventionality of his prose and for the mystical, telluric quality, at once brutal and tender, of his stories.

José Carlos Cavalcanti Borges

With God's Blessing, Mom

I

My dear son,

Your father's headache is a little better. Mr. Quincas, the new druggist at the corner, says it might be albumen. What do you think?

Someone told me that you're going with a girl. They said it was serious.

My son, I don't think it is time yet for you to get involved with anyone. Your father and I talked it over and he thinks just as I do. You haven't graduated yet. Even after graduation you'll find that life is very difficult nowadays. I didn't really believe it about you and this girl being serious. But anyway, don't be angry with me for offering a bit of advice.

Little Bernardo has been studying more. The teacher says he seems to be developing a taste for it. (But I wish he wasn't so crazy about music. He goes to all the band rehearsals at the Euterpe Club.)

Do you think it would help your father if he went to Recife for an examination?

Be sensible, my son.

With God's blessing,
Mom

II

My dear son,

I was greatly relieved by what you wrote in your letter. Everybody here has been catching the grippe. I'm glad to say that your father's headache is no worse. He had a touch of the grippe, but it was mostly in the nose.

The person who told me about your girl must have thought it was true. I trust her implicitly. She is the sister of a lady who lives near you. She wouldn't tell me the girl's name but she said it was someone I was acquainted with and that if I knew the whole truth I wouldn't like it.

But now I'm happy. I know it's not what she thinks and that it's nothing but a silly flirtation.

Be careful, my son. You aren't rich. Your father is advanced in years and his greatest happiness would be to see you graduated and with a good job. My greatest happiness, too.

Mr. Quincas offered to bring it to you, and so I'm taking advantage of his kindness to send you this dried beef. It was bought on Saturday. Your father picked the kind you like.

I almost forgot the big news. The mayor said he was going to open a school and promised Ceminha a job as teacher. She is very happy. So are we.

With God's blessing,
Mom

III

My dear son,

It's two weeks since I last wrote you. Ceminha has the grippe. Little Bernardo got a bad cold. He caught it one night when it was raining and he went to a rehearsal at the Euterpe Club. Your father forbade him to go any more until he's older.

You said it wasn't at all important about you and Lélé, but I'm wondering if you yourself realize how serious it might be. Going to the movies with her. Walking on the beach with her as if you were engaged.

Is it really not serious, my son?

You may be very fond of her. But, my son, I'm going to speak frankly, because I'm your mother. Don't you know what people here and in Recife say about Lélé's mother? There are so many girls and you have to pick Palmira's daughter. Don't you know that Palmira is practically separated from her husband? The only reason he doesn't actually leave her is that she has money. Her daughter may have many good points but, after all, she lives with her mother, she was brought up by her mother, and she must have learned her mother's ways. The girl may like you and may seem very nice, but later on she will probably turn out bad like her mother. I'm speaking to you frankly.

Your father says that Ceminha's job in the school is definite. I'm not so sure. I don't trust these politicians.

Think carefully about what I told you. Would you really want to marry into Palmira's family?

With God's blessing,

Mom

IV

My dear son,

I have been crying. Even your father is becoming suspicious. You write one thing but you do something else. Do you think people here don't know what goes on in Recife? Well, you're very much mistaken. You've been going swimming at the beach with Lélé. You've been walking on Nova Street with her and her mother, as if you were officially engaged already. All that's missing is the ring. My son, do you want to ruin your life? Don't you see that this attachment is not right for you? I made a promise to the good Lord of what I'll do if He saves you. I'm sure He will.

Tomorrow or the day after, the postmaster's sister is going to Recife to spend a few days. I'm going to take advantage of the opportunity to send you some cookies. If they are soggy when they get there, ask permission to put them in the stove for a few minutes and they'll get nice and crisp.

Why don't you spend more time studying that subject in which you got a low grade?

My son, I write you with tears in my eyes, for I know what you have in store for you. Don't have anything more to do with that girl. She will ruin your life, my son.

With God's blessing,

Mom

V

My dear son,

I sent the cookies as I promised. Remember what to do if they're soggy. Your father woke up this morning with a terrible headache. Don't have anything more to do with that girl.

With God's blessing,

Mom

VI

My dear son,

Your father is somewhat better. He has been going out and working. Sometimes around noon when the sun is very hot, his head bothers him. Quincas says that if he goes to a doctor in Recife he'll find out it's albumen.

Aren't you convinced yet, my son, that the girl is no good for you? How can you be so blind? If I believed in spiritism I would think a spell had been cast upon you. I worry about it a great deal and it makes me very sad. But God will not desert me. He raised Lazarus from the dead and He can save you from this girl.

The music teacher asked your father to let little Bernardo take lessons. He says the boy has a fine sense of rhythm. He can take lessons during the day, after school. What do you think?

Ceminha is still waiting for her appointment as teacher. The mayor rented a nice house for the school, on the Street of the Matriz. You remember where Francisca used to live? Well, that's the house.

I know you are still seeing that girl. A friend of mine saw you in a café drinking with her and Palmira. Have you met Palmira's husband yet? My friend said you stayed in the café with them a long time. When she left, you were still there. I don't think you realize how I feel when I hear something like this. I thought—for no real reason, but nevertheless I thought—that your friendship for Lélé was almost over. So you are drinking now, my son. Don't you know what drinking does to a person? After your father has one small glass of wine he doesn't know what he's doing.

I never thought anybody like that girl could make my life so miserable. You have never before been ungrateful to me, my son. If anyone tells your father about it, I don't know what will happen. He already acts as if he suspects something.

With God's blessing,
Mom

P.S. Grandma wants me to ask you if you know a good medicine for rheumatism. In her feet.

VII

My dear son,

I was happy to get your letter. I know now that you haven't forgotten your mother entirely. But I notice you don't say anything about you and that brazen-faced girl. I am worried, my son. If you don't want to tell me about it, it must be serious. (I heard that Palmira's husband left for Rio de Janeiro. I don't know whether it's true.) Why don't you write me about you and the girl?

Take your mother's advice, my son. All that I want in the whole world is your happiness.

Yesterday I felt terribly ashamed. At the novena, Maria Pia came up and asked me if you were getting married to Palmira's daughter. She heard it somewhere. I didn't know what to say. All through the novena and all night long I sobbed until I nearly choked. I tell you this because you ought to know how I am suffering.

You must not think that your father and I don't want you to fall in love and get married. But a boy like you deserves a different kind of girl, a fine girl, a girl of good upbringing. Besides, isn't it a little early for you to be thinking of marriage? Don't let yourself become engaged to that girl, my son. It's for your own good, believe me.

Little Bernardo wants you to buy "The Art of Music" for him to study. He says they have it in the bookstores in Recife. Your father will send you the money as soon as he knows of someone going to Recife.

May the good Lord watch over you, my son.

Mom

VIII

My dear son,

For the past three days your father has been unable to sleep. His head hurts him all the time. Mr. Quincas doesn't want him to take any more aspirin. Your father hardly eats a thing.

I found out something very sad today—your father knows everything. He has been worrying in silence for a long time without saying a word to me about it. Yesterday, when your letter came, he asked me to read it to him. His migraine is so bad he can't focus his eyes. When I finished, he said, "I was beginning to feel a little better, Iáiá, because something told me that in that letter João would tell us he had broken off with that brazen-faced girl."

Poor man! I felt so sorry for him. I had never mentioned the subject to him because I wanted your father to get well.

Ceminha has been helping me a great deal. She was studying to begin her teaching but these days she has no time for it.

Do you know of any medicine that might help your father? He won't take injections. Mr. Quincas means well but his drug store is worse than when Mr. Lobo was there.

I can't wait for the holidays to come, my son.

With God's blessing,
Mom

IX

My dear son,

We're all so happy here to learn that you're coming on the first of December. It is the most joyful news we could have.

Is it really true, my son? Is your friendship for Lélé and Palmira really not serious?

Today the mayor was at the internal revenue office and he spoke to your father. He was very roundabout, but the gist of it was that he isn't going to appoint Ceminha as teacher in the new school. He had a request from a municipal judge who wanted the job for his niece. You don't know her, she came to live here only about a month ago. The judge has a cousin who was a congressman. The mayor promised to have a position for Ceminha in another school that he's going to open next year near the slaughterhouse.

Little Bernardo is already accompanying the band on his trumpet. Your father pretends he doesn't approve, but almost every night he stands at the door of the Euterpe Club and listens.

Is it really not serious, my son?

Study hardest the subjects in which you are weakest.

I hear that neckties with a solid color are the thing to wear now. I've been saving a piece of blue silk. It's very pretty. For

a lining I'll use one that I took from an old necktie of your
father's.

With God's blessing,
Mom

I put this letter in an envelope, but luckily I did not seal it.
This evening when your father got back from the Euterpe, he
found Ceminha talking with a young man. He didn't say anything to her but he wasn't happy about it and he told me he was
going to find out who the young man is. Tomorrow I'll have a
talk with her.

Mom

* * *

JOSÉ CARLOS CAVALCANTI BORGES was born in 1910 in Goiana,
Pernambuco, and lives in Recife, capital of the state. He is a physician specializing in psychiatry. Since 1958 he has lectured on
psychology at the Federal University of Recife in a course of studies
for the stage.

Dr. Borges has written three books of short stories and a number
of plays, several of which have been produced. Critics have remarked his ability to capture the Brazilian northeast in both idiom
and ways of thinking. He is a member of the Pernambucan Academy
of Letters.

"With God's Blessing, Mom" (Coração de D. Iáiá") is from his
first book, *Neblina,* 1940.

Darcy Azambuja

At the Side of the Road

Every traveler who has passed along Black Hill Road, lost in its course of many leagues through the countryside, knows the house of old Chico Pedro. It is located on one of the knolls which, on that plateau, raise the surface of the fields in undulations like immense, round stones covered by a green carpet. From afar one can see the white house, always happy and bright between the fig trees plump as cabbages and the crowns of the orange trees flourishing in the back yard. On one side, spilling over the small picket fence and perfuming the air, there blossomed in spring and summer a lovely trellised vine of honeysuckles. On the other side, skirting the garden hedge, a little road ran down to the spring, Chico Pedro's famous water hole. In front of the house, where it is shady in the afternoon, there used to be a bench against the wall, and there, whenever the weather was pleasant, sat old Chico Pedro in shirtsleeves, a kettle at his side, drinking maté and smoking. Passers-by were used to seeing that peaceful figure of an old gaucho—an octogenarian, by his own report—and very few of them had not shared a maté with him. His house, the only one within a radius of four or five leagues, was a bit of divine providence in that vast stretch of open country. A traveling salesman whose mule went lame, a wagoner with tired horses or a broken harness, a driver of pack animals seeking an enclosure for them—all, known or unknown, turned to old Chico Pedro and were taken care of. And when the person expressed his gratitude and started to leave, Chica Pedro's wife would come with a cup of coffee and a slice of melon if the weather was warm or a small glass of palm cordial in winter. Everything free, just to be pleasant and helpful; and as one could see, it was only in being pleasant and helpful that he was rewarded.

Now and then someone would say:

"But Mr. Chico Pedro, this isn't right. Tell me how much I owe you for the new harness strap."

"Forget it, friend, it's not worth anything. Some day I'll need something and you'll help me."

Another would say:

"Mr. Chico Pedro, I don't know when I'll be able to send the horse back to you. Let's make a deal: how much will you take for him?"

"No, friend, he's not worth anything. When you get to the village just turn him loose and he'll come right home."

His liberality often made him a prey to the unscrupulous. Even so, he never turned anyone down who looked to him for help.

In the winter, late in the cold, rainy nights, travelers who had been delayed by the swollen fords would knock at his door. They were immediately welcomed, their horses let loose in the corral, their vehicles sheltered in the shed. And the kind old lady of the house, although always ailing, would get up and come with steaming hot coffee for the half-frozen guests.

"Don't ever hesitate, friends," Chico Pedro would say the following morning. "Next time you come by, drop in for a maté."

And they would start on their way, happy and warm from his open-handed hospitality and, indeed, already longing to return. It was with deep attachment that they would look back at the old man with his wide, loose gaucho trousers held tight at the waist by a leather belt, a maté gourd in his hand, his pure white hair, his beard scattered on his chest, waving affectionately to his friends of a day.

Good old Chico Pedro . . .

For some time, however, a shadow of sorrow had darkened that life, previously as serene as a stream running over a bed of sand. He seemed dispirited, almost never joined in a conversation.

Because of his son.

His one descendant, the only offspring of his long life, was filling the final years of this life with grief and shame.

That morning, seated on the wooden bench and drinking maté, he gazed long at the light-green fields losing themselves in the distance. The sun was climbing in the deep sky, whose blue was interrupted only by a long, thin cloud, a jet of white vapor. Cattle grazed peacefully on the knolls nearby, and a little flock of ewes formed a white patch in the bottom land to the right of the house. The crickets chirped shrilly in the bushes and in the honeysuckle trellis. From the cherry trees around the water hole came the sad cooing of doves. A rooster in the yard cackled intermittently. Birds were flying about in the light.

All the sweetness of summer's end smiled in the clear air. From time to time, one of the two fig trees, immobile, contemplative, let a dry leaf fall like a dead thought.

Old Chico Pedro drank his maté and slowly took in the countryside, which for eighty years had filled his rustic soul with tranquility. He drank his maté and mulled over the facts that were now the burden of his old age.

How had it happened? Why had such a bad colt issued from him, who had always been a decent man, and from the old lady, who was a saint? Their son, so quiet and obedient when small, had turned into a bandit! . . . It seemed a great lie. . . . It all happened after he enlisted. Bad companions . . . During his stretch in the army he was always being arrested for brawling. After he was mustered out he became worse. He never went home again, never wanted to know anything about his parents. He began to roam the country, to drink, to gamble. And then came that succession of evil, shameful crimes. In the first of his really savage fights, he killed a wagoner and one of his eyes was gouged out. He spent four years in prison, and from then on he was Johnny One-Eye, the gambler and hoodlum. He was always surrounded by an ugly gang of hangers-on. Although watched by the police, he got into fights, especially at race tracks and in bars. Scarcely a month passed in which Chico Pedro did not receive news of some brawl or swindle in which his son was involved. How it pained the old man, who in all his long existence had never done a shameful thing and who was loved and respected by all.

Finally, Johnny One-Eye committed one crime too many, murdering the father of a girl he had wronged. And he fled to Uruguay, where he remained more than six years. It was better so; at least the old man had a respite. Now, however, with the revolution, Johnny One-Eye had returned, and his vicious exploits were on everyone's lips. Whenever the force to which he belonged passed through that part of the country, it left a trail of cruelty and terror. People told of the cold-bloodedness with which he murdered, plundered, raped, committed every sort of barbarity. Similar reports came from other places. Travelers, taking maté with Chico Pedro, talked about the mandatory subject of conversation—the revolution—and, apropos, brought news of some new mischief of the notorious Johnny One-Eye, for few of them knew he was the son of that kind old man. Chico Pedro always remained silent while the sad reports were given him. He had learned recently that his son had been expelled from the force to which he had been attached and had formed his own band of irregulars, which was soon steeped in new cruelties. A week ago he had attacked a ranch and had cut the throat of an old man in the presence of his wife and two daughters, who had been tied and forced to watch. One of the women had gone mad. . . .

These and other stories with which travelers unintentionally wounded him, tortured old Chico Pedro with grief and shame to such a point that he felt apprehensive when anyone approached the house, which nevertheless remained always open and hospitable. He had done everything possible to hide these terrible things from his wife; but, inevitably, the poor old lady had learned all. She wept continually now and was failing and dying of pure grief. . . .

And thinking thus about the black shadow on his life, Chico Pedro spent more than an hour sipping his maté and smoking straw cigarettes. His wife, bent over, her hair as white as cotton, came out of the house and placed her leather-covered stool near the door. She sat there without a word, her head down over her sewing. She and her husband remained a long time in silence, the silence of people who have passed their lives together and who speak and understand without words.

In the quiet, delicate morning air, the honeysuckle perfume rose and was gently diffused. The crickets continued their frenzied song.

A little later, lapwings sang on the nearby knoll over which the road passed, and a traveler appeared. He wore a white poncho, rode a bay horse at a slow trot, and headed toward the house.

Chico Pedro recognized him immediately. It was Zeferino, of High Slope, doubtless on his way to the village.

As his wife withdrew into the house, Chico Pedro said to her:

"Have the boy get the kettle and the gourd for some fresh maté."

Soon the traveler arrived and tied his horse by the halter to the metal ring on one of the fig trees.

"Good afternoon, Chico Pedro. How are you?"

"Fine and at your service. How is my friend?"

And they embraced. Zeferino sat down on the chair that the old man pushed toward him, threw his poncho over one shoulder, and began to chat. At first they talked about the drought, which the recent rains had ended, then about the disease that was spreading among the cattle, and, finally, about the obligatory subject. The visitor told whatever news and rumors he had heard. He told about battles, the death of some mutual friend, and the general opinion that the civil war would last a long time.

A little colored boy came with the kettle and the gourd, delivered them to the old man, and extended his hand to Zeferino:

"Give me your blessing, sir."

"May God bless you, my Negro."

While the host carefully prepared the first maté, Zeferino was saying:

"The day before yesterday there was a fight up at High Slope, near the ford."

"Hm! What troops were they?"

"I don't know for sure, but I saw the whole thing. I was with Lautério, going the rounds of the ranch boundaries. On that hill to the right of the road, near the ford—you know where I mean, don't you?—we saw an encampment at the edge of the woods where the spring is. A small force, just a patrol of thirty men more or less. We were trying to make out who they were, when we noticed another force, maybe two hundred, coming from the direction of the winter pasture and cutting through the wire fence. It kept coming on, sneaking up like a cat under the protection of the hillside, and it was less than twelve meters away when the sentinel of the camp realized what was happening. The smaller force quickly mounted their horses, crossed the ford, and entrenched themselves on the other side. You know the ford, how narrow it is.

"Lautério and I watched the thing from a distance, on top of the hill. And then a funny thing happened. Along the road came Moisés, the Arab, with his pack mule in front of him, headed straight for the ford. He seemed real tired and I guess he hadn't noticed anything. When the first shots were fired, he jumped on the mule, which set off like crazy, peddling boxes of buttons and pieces of madras to the winds. . . .

"The troops that had come up, relying on their greater number, dashed forward as if they wanted to cross the ford, but the patrol popped bullets at them, only it was no kids' game. And that's how they were, shooting from this side, shooting from the other side, until it got dark.

"Then the larger force divided itself in two. One part went on covering the ford with its fire; the other part slowly went down by the edge of the woods, looking for a place to cross the river further downstream so they could attack from behind. And undoubtedly that's what happened, only we didn't see it because night was coming on and we went back home. But around nine o'clock we heard a steady gunfire that lasted a long time and then suddenly stopped. That must have been when they began to fight hand to hand."

Old Chico Pedro was listening to the story half interested, half fearful with a vague presentiment.

"Yesterday morning, when I went back there, Lautério and Claro came with me to look at the place where the battle had been. And it was a sad sight, I can tell you.

"We found a big grave, in which more than ten men must have been buried, and, inside the woods, behind the gullies, there were pools of dried blood, dead horses, hats, a rifle, and other wreckage of the battle. And a sad thing . . . We were just leaving when we noticed, on a little rise, an unburied body that had been left stretched out there as a sort of warning.

"We went up and saw that it had been staked to the ground, with the head almost separated from the shoulders. What barbarity! It gave me a sick feeling.

"But when Lautério and Claro said who it was—God forgive me!—I felt that it served him right. It was that Johnny One-Eye. After all . . ."

At this point Zeferino was interrupted, for Chico Pedro, who had been pouring the maté, dropped the gourd, burning his hands with the hot water.

"Hey, Chico, what happened?"

The old man looked down, wiped his hands on his large checkered handkerchief, and answered in a low voice:

"It's nothing, friend. . . .

"It's nothing, but it's enough to bring tears to your eyes! Put olive oil on it and I guarantee the pain will go away."

"No, really, it doesn't amount to anything. . . ."

And, wrapping his hand in the handkerchief, he said:

"Speak softly, because the old lady's in there and she gets all upset with these stories about the war."

But it was too late, for at that very moment they heard from within the house a stifled, anguished sob.

And no one could understand why, from that day on, old Chico Pedro never again sat in front of the house sipping his maté. Even the honeysuckles, for lack of care, began to wither.

For one year more he took care of travelers.

As a new winter began, his wife died, and the last honeysuckle vine had not yet flowered when they buried Chico Pedro next to the grave of his companion, under a calabash tree in back of the house. The flowers of the calabash are precocious: they are born and soon fall. As early as November they heap the ground with purple petals and deck the two graves, something that the hands of friends cannot be expected to do in that solitary place.

The property fell to a distant relative, who rented out the fields and did not bother with the house.

Today, anyone who passes can see that it is closed, that it shelters no one. The wooden bench has disappeared. The honeysuckle trellis has fallen and so have the picket fences. After the rains and winds finish with the roof—there is already a big hole in it—they will knock down a wall, the doors, the windows. . . . And slowly the house will become a ruin, a peaceful ruin, where insects and worms will always find a welcome.

And, finally, even the debris will slowly merge into the green earth, like the lives of the two good people who spent almost a century there.

But the two fig trees will remain and, in back, so will the calabash tree, laying its purple flowers on the two forgotten graves.

* * *

DARCY PEREIRA DE AZAMBUJA was born in 1903 in the town of Encruzilhada, Rio Grande do Sul. He was graduated from law school in Porto Alegre. Subsequently he held various state offices, including those of public prosecutor, attorney general, and secretary of the Interior and Justice. At present he is a professor in the schools of law and philosophy of the University of Rio Grande do Sul and in the coresponding schools of a Catholic university.

He has written several books on political theory as well as three volumes of short stories. "At the Side of the Road" ("Beira de Estrada") is from his first book, *No Galpão,* published in 1925 and considered a milestone in the history of the regional literature of the Far South.

Clarice Lispector

The Crime of the Mathematics Professor

When the man reached the top of the highest hill, bells were tolling in the city below him. Nothing could be clearly distinguished but the irregular roofs of the houses. The man stood there, near the only tree on the hilltop. He was holding a heavy bag.

He looked down myopically at the tiny Catholics slowly entering the church and tried to hear the voices of the children scattered about the square. The morning was clear, yet the sounds barely reached the hilltop. He looked down also at the river, which seemed motionless, and he thought: it is Sunday. He could see in the distance the high mountain with its arid cliffs. Although the air was not cold, he turned up his collar. Finally, he placed the bag carefully on the ground. Then he took off his glasses, apparently to breathe more freely, for with the glasses in his hand he inhaled deeply. The bright light hit the lenses, glancing off in sharp signals. Without the glasses the man's eyes twinkled and looked younger. He put the glasses on, returning to middle age, and picked up the bag.

"It is heavy as stone," he thought.

He strained his eyes to see the flow of the river; he inclined his head to hear better: the river remained motionless and only the shrillest voice suceeded, momentarily, in reaching the height. Yes, he was quite alone. The cool air seemed inhospitable, for he had lived in the greater warmth of the city. He stood looking at the lone tree, whose branches were swaying. After a time, he decided there was no reason to put it off any longer.

Nevertheless, he continued to procrastinate. Obviously his glasses bothered him, for he took them off again, breathed deeply, and put them in his pocket.

Then he opened the bag, inserted a thin hand, and pulled out the dead dog. His whole being was concentrated on that hand, and he kept his eyes tightly shut. When he opened them, the air was even clearer and the merry bells were calling the faithful to the comfort of punishment.

The unknown dog lay in full view.

The man began working methodically. He picked up the dog, black and stiff, and placed him in a little declivity of the earth. But, as though he had already accomplished a great deal, he put on his glasses, sat down beside the dog, and looked about.

He contemplated the empty hilltop with a certain futility. Seated as he was, he could no longer see the little city below. He breathed deeply again. He reached into the bag and pulled out a shovel. He thought about the choice of a place. It could be right there under the tree. This idea disturbed him. If it had been the other, the real dog, he would have buried him where he himself would have liked to be buried—in the very center of the hilltop, facing the sun with empty eyes. The unknown dog was a substitute and, in order to perfect the act, he wanted to give him exactly the same treatment the other would have received. There was no confusion in the man's mind. He understood himself coldly, consistently.

He tried scrupulously to ascertain the exact center of the hilltop. This was not easy, for the lone tree stood to one side, setting itself up as a false center and dividing the area asymmetrically.

"I really don't have to bury him in the center," the man conceded, "for I might well have buried the other anywhere, perhaps at the spot where I am now standing."

He wanted to give the act the fatality of mere chance, the stamp of a plain and external event, in the same category as the children in the square or the Catholics entering the church. It all had to be utterly visible, right there on the surface of the earth under the sky. The act and he himself had to be freed from the remoteness and impunity of a thought.

The mere idea of burying the dog at the spot where he was standing caused the man to jump backward with an agility unsuited to his small but singularly heavy body. For he seemed to see the dog's grave beneath his feet.

He began digging rhythmically. Sometimes he stopped to take

off his glasses and put them on again. He perspired profusely. The grave was shallow, not because he wanted to spare himself but because the thought occurred to him:

"If it were for the real dog, it would not be deep. I would bury him as near the surface as possible."

He believed that the dog, with very little earth above him, would not lose the power of sensation.

Finally he put the shovel down, gently picked up the unknown dog, and placed him in the grave.

What a strange face the dog had! When, with a shock, he had come upon the dog, dead on a street corner, the idea of burying him had so astonished and weighed upon his heart that he had not even noticed this hard nose and dried drivel. It was an alien and objective dog.

The body was slightly bigger than the hole. The grave would be a barely perceptible protuberance on the hilltop. That was the way he wanted it. He covered the dog with earth and smoothed the surface with his hands, pleasurably feeling the dog's shape in his palms as though he were caressing the animal. The dog was now part of the terrain. The man rose, shook the earth from his hands, and looked away from the grave. He thought, with a certain pleasure:

"I have done it."

He sighed. An innocent smile of liberation appeared on his face. Yes, he had done everything. His crime had been punished and he was free.

Now at last he could think of the real dog without constraint. The real dog who right now must be wandering, puzzled, sniffing through the streets of the other city, where he had no owner.

He concentrated his thoughts on the real dog as if on his own life. His bittersweet affection for the animal helped to overcome the handicap of distance.

"While I was making you in my image, you were making me in yours," he thought. "I called you Joseph so that your name could serve you also as a soul. And you—how can I ever know the name you gave me with your great love, greater, I'm afraid, than my love for you.

"We understood each other too well, you with the human

name I gave you, I with the name you told me only by your insistent look." The man smiled affectionately, free now to recollect at will.

"I remember when you were small and weak. How funny you were then! You would wag your tail and look at me, while I was discovering in you a new way of knowing my soul. Yet even then, day by day, you were growing into a dog that could be utterly forsaken. Meanwhile, our games were becoming dangerous because of our excess of mutual understanding." The man recalled this with satisfaction. "They always ended with you biting me and grumbling and with me throwing a book at you and laughing. But my laughter was forced. And who can say what it may already have meant. You were a dog that could be forsaken at any time.

"How you used to sniff the streets!" thought the man, with a faint smile. "Really, not a single stone escaped your investigation. . . . This was your childish side. Or was it just your obligation as a dog? And, for the rest, were you merely playing at being mine? For you were unconquerable. Wagging your tail calmly, you seemed silently to reject the name I had given you. Oh, yes, you were unconquerable. I did not want you to eat meat lest it make you ferocious. But one day you jumped on the table and, amidst the happy shrills of the children, snapped up the roast. With a fierceness that does not come from what is eaten, you glared at me mute and unyielding, with the meat in your mouth. For, although mine, you never relinquished, even a little, your past or your nature. And, apprehensive, I began to understand that I did not have to relinquish any part of my own self for you to love me, and this was beginning to trouble me. You expected us to reach a mutual understanding on the basis of the resistant reality of our two natures. Neither my ferocity nor yours should be changed into gentleness: this is what you were gradually teaching me and it was becoming burdensome. Without asking for anything, you asked for too much. From you I demanded your being a dog, from me you demanded that I be a man. And I pretended as well as I could. Sometimes, sitting before me, how you stared at my face! I would look at the ceiling, cough, examine my fingernails. But you would not take your eyes off me. Whom might you tell what you discovered? I would say to myself: 'Pretend quickly that you are someone else, deceive him, pat him, throw him a bone.' But nothing would divert your attention: you kept staring at me. I was a fool. I trembled with horror, while you were the innocent one. What if I had turned suddenly and shown you my real face? I know what you would have done. You would have got up and gone to the door, bristling, deeply hurt. Oh, you were a dog that could be forsaken at any time. I could choose. Yet you wagged your tail with self-assurance.

"Sometimes, in retaliation, I perceived your own anguish. Not the anguish of being a dog, for this was your only possible form, but the anguish of existing in so perfect a way that it became an unbearable happiness. Then you would jump on my lap and lick my face with a completely surrendered love and with a dangerous element of hate, as though it had been I, through my friendship, who had found you out. I can see clearly now that it was not I who had a dog: it was you who had a person.

"But you had a person powerful enough to choose, and he chose to desert you. He deserted you and felt relief. Yes, relief, for you demanded, with the simple, calm incomprehension of a heroic dog, that I be a man. I deserted you with an excuse approved by everyone in the household: how could I move from one city to another with my family and all my belongings and take a dog along, too! With all the problems of adapting to a new school and a new city, why should I burden myself with a dog! 'Which will only be in the way,' said Martha sensibly. 'Which will annoy the passengers,' said my mother-in-law, unintentionally helping me to justify myself. The children cried but I turned away from them. Nor did I look at you, Joseph. Only the two of us know why I deserted you: because you represented the constant possibility of the crime I never committed. The possibility of my sinning, which, in my eyes, was already a sin. So I sinned immediately in order to be immediately guilty. And this crime took the place of the greater one that I lacked the courage to commit." So thought the man, with ever increasing clarity.

"There are so many ways of being guilty and damning yourself forever, of betraying yourself, of evading yourself," he continued. "I chose to hurt a dog. For I knew that this crime was considered petty. I knew that no one would be consigned to hell for deserting a dog who had trusted him. I knew my crime was unpunishable."

As the man sat there on the hilltop, his mathematical mind was cold and rational. Now at last, its icy plenitude enabled him to see clearly that what he had done to the dog would be eternally impune. For no one has ever devised a punishment for the great crimes in disguise and for the deep treasons.

A man could still manage to outsmart the Final Judgment. No one would accuse him of this crime. Not even the Church.

"They are all accessories, Joseph. If I knocked on every door and begged them to convict me, to punish me, they would scowl and slam the doors in my face. No one condemns me for my crime. Not even you, Joseph. For if this powerful person that I am chose to call you back, you would jump up and lick my face with joy and forgiveness. I would turn the other cheek for you to kiss."

The man took off his glasses, breathed deeply, and put them on again.

He looked at the covered grave. There he had buried an unknown dog as a tribute to the forsaken one, trying in this way to pay the debt with which, alarmingly, no one would charge him. Trying to punish himself with an act of kindness and thus free himself of his crime. As a man drops a dime in a hat so that he may feel free to eat his cake, although the cake is the cause of the beggar's lack of bread.

But as if Joseph were demanding of him much more than a lie; as if the dog were demanding that, by a last desperate effort, he be a man and assume full responsibility for his crime, he stared at the grave where he had buried his own weakness.

And now, more mathematical than ever, he looked for a way to erase his redemption. He would not be solaced. He bent over and solemnly, calmly, with simple movements, uncovered the dog. It looked unfamiliar with earth on its lashes and with its open, glazed eyes. Thus, the mathematics professor renewed his crime eternally. He looked to the sky and to the earth around him, asking them to witness what he had just done. Then he started down the hill toward the little city below.

*   *   *

CLARICE LISPECTOR was born in 1922 in Russia. At the age of two months she arrived with her parents in Recife, Pernambuco, where she spent her childhood. At the age of twelve she moved to Rio de Janeiro. Prior to her graduation from law school in 1944 she had worked as an editor, translator, and journalist, had begun her first novel, and had married. With her diplomat husband she lived in various countries, including the United States, where they stayed eight years. (They have separated.)

In addition to her short stories, Clarice Lispector has written five novels, one of which will be published in 1967 in English translation. Her works are noted for their profound and sometimes mysterious subjectivity.

"The Crime of the Mathematics Professor" ("O Crime do Professor de Matemática") was written originally in the 1940's, revised in 1954–1955, and included in the book *Laços de Família,* 1960.

Sun

The train stopped. The fat man reached for his valise.

"What a God-forsaken place!" he heard someone say.

He turned in the direction of the speaker. Through his tinted eyeglasses he saw an old lady, her mummy-like face wrapped in a dusty shawl. She was staring out the window.

"It looks like a graveyard," she said, and clucked her tongue ominously.

The flatness of the scorched tableland was broken by naked rocks, white as marble, which rose vertically and were nearly alike. They were the tombstones in the cemetery, mused the fat man. The sun set them aglow with stunning brightness.

The fat man took off his duster and moved through the crowded car onto the platform. The dazzling sun made him sway a little and close his eyes. After a bit, he gradually opened them again as his sight became slowly accustomed to the brightness. He got off the train. The station before him was almost in ruins. Some of the letters in the name of the place were missing. Fagots were piled at the side of the track. A wave of beggars assaulted the train, calling attention to their sores and deformities. Sitting on the ground in a shady spot and leaning against barrels, some Negroes looked indifferently at the fat man.

"What filth!" he muttered between his teeth.

The bitter taste of bile rose from his stomach, hunger gnawed at his entrails, and he felt overpowered by the heat. The locomotive emitted a moo. The chorus of beggars became more urgent. The station master appeared, wearing an old military cap and wooden slippers attached to his feet by leather thongs. He rang his hand bell. The air filled with the squeaks of air brakes, the grating of iron, and snorts from the locomotive. Laboring for breath, the train dragged itself off through the hot scrubland.

A cloud of dust ended the fat man's inertia. He coughed and picked up his valise. He passed through the group of Negroes, who continued to gaze at him indolently. At the telegraph operator's window, he leaned over and spoke:

"Which way to town?"

An anemic young man with a sparse mustache, his hair pasted down with vaseline, raised his yellowish eyes from his telegraph apparatus. He pointed by protruding his lower lip in the direction intended.

"Follow that road and you can't miss it."

"Isn't there anyone who can carry my valise?" asked the fat man irritably.

The telegraph operator looked distressed. Then suddenly he opened his mouth and tried to shout, but, although the muscles of his throat tightened, all that came out was a weak "Hey, Zé!" One of the Negroes stirred, waited a couple of minutes before getting up, rubbed his eyes, adjusted his ragged trousers, and walked four or five steps toward the telegrapher's window.

"Yes, suh?"

"You want to earn a little money?"

"Well, you know . . ."

"Carry this grip into town."

The Negro made no reply. He waited till the stranger started to walk. Then he picked up the valise and followed, limping like a dog with a dislocated hip.

They set off down the road. The fat man loosened his necktie. He took off his jacket and folded it over his arm. With his handkerchief he repeatedly mopped his face, his neck, and his bald head. Sweat made a pulp of his starched collar. The sun was punishing him. He thought he had never felt so miserable in his whole life. Everything around was brutish, aggressive. No sheltering trees, no shade whatever, to soften the hostility of the countryside. The few cacti that he saw were small and brown; they looked like pieces of dried excrement. Not far from the road, some of the massive rocks that he had observed from the train rose up with an energy that was somehow depressing. The sun seemed to be boiling the earth, and the steam made the air hot and hard to breathe. An unbroken silence, unmerciful like the sun, pervaded everything. And with every step the fat man felt that he was losing a bit of himself and that it was being integrated into the primitive brutality of that alien, scorched region.

From a slight rise in the road, he saw the town. It had only one street, which curved like a snake, following the meanderings of a thin, dark, motionless stream. He could discern no sign of life. No people, no animals. Not even a wisp of smoke from a chimney. He walked on. He saw barrels near the doors, an ox cart with no oxen, faded clothes in the yards, agricultural implements scattered at random. Everything seemed abandoned, as if a war or a plague had killed all the inhabitants.

The fat man entered the town's only hostelry, a sort of boardinghouse, which had been surrendered to the flies and the silence. The Negro put the valise down; his arms hung limply at his sides and his tongue was protruding. The fat man paid him. Then he clapped his hands. A door opened and an old mulatto woman came out, rubbing her eyes. Disconcerted by the presence of the stranger, she made a great show of straightening her disheveled hair and asked that her appearance be excused, she hadn't known that anyone was there. He interrupted her and engaged a room for three days. He asked if she could serve him lunch; he would faint if he didn't have something to eat pretty soon. The woman became upset again; she had nothing she could give him, there were no other guests, there rarely were any guests.

"But don't *you* eat?" said the fat man impatiently.

"If you wouldn't feel bad eating the kind of food that poor people . . ."

She brought him a piece of dried meat fried in pork fat, some manioc mush, two eggs, and onions. The fat man devoured everything. For dessert he had bananas.

Even in the house, the heat tyrannized everyone and everything. It was as if the sun had poured molten lead on the roof of the boardinghouse. The stranger took off his clothes. Completely naked, he stretched out on the bed. He wanted to sleep, he had to sleep. A morbid drowsiness pressed heavily on his eyes and deadened his brain. The heat never let up. The accumulated dust of the trip clogged his pores. Insects were buzzing about, settling on him, stinging him. His bloated stomach struggled to digest the heavy food. He twisted and turned. At times he felt dizzy, nauseous. He would raise himself on his elbows, with his eyes shut and his head limp with somnolence, and would belch violently. Finally he lay still. But his sleep was agitated and anguished. He was slowly being immersed in the dark, stagnant stream. He felt the contact of the brackish, sticky water, hot from the sun. He did not try to get out, he had not the strength to get out. The sun invaded his head, paralyzing his will, tormenting his brain. The water licked his skin like the tongues of a thousand slimy serpents. He became aware of the snails living in the muddy bed of the stream; they woke and spouted battalions of the fierce, wormlike parasites that cause schistosomiasis. Suddenly, with horror and revulsion, the fat man realized that his body had become a pulpy, writhing mass of these little killers.

Inundated with sweat, he woke and frightened away the crowd of insects that had been feasting upon him. He got up. There was a bitter taste in his mouth, and his tongue felt dirty. He opened his valise, took out the bottle of fruit salts, prepared a double dose, and drank it. He looked at his watch. Then he put on his pyjamas and called the woman who owned the boarding-house. Could he have a bath? There was no running water and no shower. She poured some cold water for him in a sort of vat or tub, a most unsatisfactory bath. He returned to his room and decided to finish his business in the town as quickly as possible.

It was not yet three o'clock when the fat man went out. He had on a hat, a necktie, and eyeglasses, and he wore a clean shirt and a clean linen suit. The community was starting to bestir itself. The windows of some of the houses were opened, and a woman in one of them stared at him in surprise. In the shade of a house, children were playing on the ground, mingling promiscuously with chickens and pigs. He saw the Negro who had carried his valise; the man was sitting in a cheap bar drinking away the money he had just earned. The fat man walked down the street. There was no sidewalk. The houses on either side were squat, monotonous, and generally in great disrepair. The land in front of them was not enclosed: there were no fences or walls. Now and then the stranger passed what had once been a fine house but was now abandoned and in ruins. He arrived at the Square.

"On one side of the church is City Hall," the boardinghouse woman had told him. "On the other side is the Revenue Office." The Revenue Office was still closed. The stranger knocked three times before anyone came. A dried-up man, all skin and bones, his face like a skull, opened the door. He was sucking at a straw cigarette and scowling, but his expression quickly changed. He opened the door wide as if to bid the stranger welcome. He bowed repeatedly in an excess of goodwill that left the fat man unmoved. And he apologized for having taken so long to come to the door and for the informality of his attire.

"It's this sun . . . this heat . . ."

"Yes, I understand," said the fat man as he sat down. "This sun is enough to drive anyone crazy."

"At this hour the whole town is taking a siesta. It's impossible for anybody to work here in the early afternoon."

"I'm Evaristo Peixoto," said the fat man.

"I know. I guessed it. I got word that you were coming."

"It was a dreadful trip."

"I was going to wait for you at the station. Naturally. But it seems that the train arrived on time and so everybody missed it. I think the railroad did it on purpose just to embarrass me."

"It's not important. I'm not the sort of man who insists on silly little formalities."

"Well, make yourself at home while I change my clothes."

Evaristo Peixoto opened his jacket. He took off his glasses and cleaned the green lenses meticulously. The people who lived in the house were waking. The fat man heard stifled noises, voices, a woman scolding, children crying. It made him nervous to hear children cry. He detested children. Soon the tax collector returned.

"The sooner I finish my work here, the better," said Evaristo Peixoto.

"There isn't much to be done," replied the collector. "You could see, there's not a great deal of business here. Very few taxpayers. This was once an important district, with high tax revenue. But the sun, this sun . . . You know," he added, as if speaking to himself, "sometimes I feel that my brains are melting when I go out in the street and the sun beats down on my head for ten minutes. And then there's that putrid little stream . . ."

"Yes. I saw it."

"I ought to warn you. Don't drink any water unless it's boiled first. Don't even take a bath in water unless it's been boiled."

"I wouldn't like to live here. I'd go crazy, or take to drink, or become a murderer. This sun makes you want to kill."

The collector agreed.

"There are no sane, healthy people here," he said. "Nobody can stay normal under this sun. I keep praying to God that the government will send me somewhere else, anywhere else. It can't be worse than this place."

Evaristo Peixoto, too, was thinking of himself.

"As I said, the sooner I finish my work here, the better."

The collector had sat down and had opened an enormous book of accounts.

"Not much really to do. There's only one business house here worthy of the name. The others are just little shops. No problems. Here, you can tell at a glance. There used to be lots of businesses here, lots of revenue. But the sun ruined everything. Now the district exports nothing but rum. It's funny how, with everything else going to ruin, the production of rum increased."

The two were silent awhile. Evaristo Peixoto's eyelids felt as heavy as if he had not slept for days. His head ached and felt swollen. The children's crying had stopped, but the buzzing of insects continued, a most enervating music. He wanted to let the work go till the next day. He felt, however, that if he put it off for one day he would put it off forever.

"Let's start," he said.

The two men went out. It was the middle of the afternoon. Although the sun's rays were oblique, the heat had not diminished. The shops and stalls were open and the government offices were functioning. From the little bar came the sound of billiard balls. An ox cart went creaking by, bearing a load of rum barrels. Evaristo Peixoto was soaked in sweat.

"Damned sun!" he muttered as he entered the first shop.

He worked until after the Ave Marias, using the light of a tin kerosene lamp when night fell. Even then, no relief, no refreshing breeze. The earth gave forth as a hot exhalation what it had stored during the hours of sun. When the revenue agent felt exhausted, the collector walked him back to the boardinghouse.

"Your work is nearly done. Didn't I tell you it would be a snap?"

"I can't wait to get out of here. Tomorrow I'll finish. The day after, there's a train that stops here early in the morning, isn't there?"

"If it's not late."

"I hope it's not. This town gets me down. The riffraff that live here make me nauseous."

"I used to think about the trains, too, wondering when I'd be taking one out of here." The collector looked down and murmured, "I have faith in God that the government will send me to some other place."

He said good night. Evaristo Peixoto went to bed. His whole body hurt. He tried to relax his nerves and muscles. Sleep took possession of him, but it was a sleep mutilated by dreams. The foul stream was swelling, rising, boiling from some fire within, threatening to burn him alive. The townspeople were looking on without making a gesture to save him. Then came the account books—journals, ledgers—with their records of sales for cash, sales on credit; they oppressed him, smothered him. He got up several times during the night. Bathed in sweat and breathing hard, he lit one cigarette after another, smoked them until they burned his fingers. Fully awake, he remembered the countryside as it looked from the train, with those immense white obelisks tearing upward through space and burning in the sun. And he remembered the face of the old mummy when she spoke those words of ill omen:

"It looks like a graveyard."

When he could no longer bear his anxiety, he dressed and went out into the street. He wandered about until dawn.

Barrels of rum on squeaking ox carts; ragged people around the doors of the little shops; urchins with swollen bellies eating earth; pigs, goats, and asses foraging in the street. He saw ugly, misshapen, sexless women, worn out and resigned to suffering; they were repulsive to him. The small shopkeepers interrupted their work to stare at him as if he had been some strange and odious beast. At his side the collector chattered incessantly, seeking his help in getting the government to transfer him. The revenue agent walked along, his nerves raw, cursing that sun, which, so early in the morning, was already agonizing. They stopped before a store. It had four doors, and its front had recently been painted. Its general aspect of prosperity contrasted sharply with the poverty all around it. The collector went in.

"Hi, Miguel."

"Hi," came a slender thread of a voice from a hammock behind the counter.

Evaristo Peixoto took off his glasses. He heard the hammock creak and saw someone get up from it slowly, lazily. The collector introduced them. Miguel gave no sign or word that he was glad to meet the stranger. The revenue agent was about to proffer his hand but sensed that Miguel would certainly not grasp it and desisted in time. He looked at the man from head to foot. There was not much to see. He was like a piece of spoiled fruit. Small, withered, amorphous. He looked as if he had never been a young man but had leaped from a feeble puberty to an anemic maturity. His face was yellow, drawn, chinless, and his lips were thin. The only signs of life were his large, bulging eyes, in which there were spots that betrayed an ailing liver. His rolled-up sleeves revealed arms as thin as twigs. A little protruding belly was out of keeping with the rest of his body.

Miguel threw away the straw cigarette on which he had been chewing. He did not invite the revenue agent to enter the interior part of the store; instead he ordered his only salesman to bring a chair out front. It was a deliberate expression of contempt, thought Evaristo Peixoto.

"I've been to all the other stores, Miguel. I saved yours for last because it's the most important. You deserve special treatment." There was a sneer in the revenue agent's voice. He was trying to reciprocate.

Miguel opened a large drawer. With an effort he took out some heavy books.

"Here they are," he said drily.

"I hope they're in order," bantered the agent.

The store owner's face remained impassive.

"I wouldn't like to draw up charges against you, Miguel. I had to with all the other proprietors on the Square. Except two, who begged me to forgive them; I haven't decided about them yet. You know, trading in rum on the side."

Miguel said nothing. For an instant their eyes met, and the

gaze of each of the two men seemed to penetrate the other. Evaristo Peixoto shuddered. With revulsion. There was something in this rachitic little man that stank; it exuded from his greenish skin, it floated around in his bulging eyes. The revenue agent felt as if he had a hyena before him. Exactly, a hyena. This was odd, for he had never seen a hyena. But a hyena must have been just so. And, when he made the hyena flinch a little and lower his eyes, he experienced his first satisfaction since he had got off the train. Evaristo Peixoto fixed his eyes in turn on the collector and the salesman, making them witnesses of his power. Then he sat down. The store owner returned to his hammock and shut his eyes. He curled up as if hiding from the overpowering presence of the revenue agent. The hours went by. The sun rose higher, the heat got worse. The agent worked on, listing items, checking them, adding them. The collector helped him. Curved over the books, the two men were surprisingly alike; despite their physical disparity, they looked like twins, like twin vultures.

The church bell struck twelve. Miguel slowly got out of the hammock, which creaked as he did so.

"Let's go, Nandinho!"

The salesman, who was sitting on the gas container, gave a start.

"Yes, sir." His voice was thin and weak.

Evaristo Peixoto's face flushed. He raised his eyes from the books.

"Are you going to close the store?" he asked, tapping on the counter with his pen.

"It's lunch time."

"But I haven't finished yet."

"Here, nobody works between noon and three o'clock."

The revenue agent's face turned from pink to scarlet.

"You can leave if you wish. I'm not sick. I'll go on working. Leave your salesman with me."

The store owner stood there motionless. He moved only those muscles necessary for speech:

"My salesman eats with me."

"Then I'll stay here alone."

Miguel glared at him. For the second time, he and the revenue agent dueled with their eyes.

"In my house I give the orders."

Evaristo Peixoto felt his blood turning to fire. But he saw no alternative to temporary surrender. He mastered himself.

"All right. I'll be back at three o'clock."

He tried to keep his voice calm, but he felt that the little man had avenged himself. When he got to the door, he saw a group of curious onlookers scurrying away; he had not known they were there. He did not go back to the boardinghouse, for the tax collector had invited him to lunch. Evaristo Peixoto could not enjoy the meal. The depressing company of the collector, the ridiculously ceremonious manner of his faded wife, their sickly, quarrelsome children, took his appetite away. After lunch the collector and his wife, eager to please, ushered him into the parlor and made conversation with him. He would have preferred a little nap. As soon as the clock struck three, he put on his jacket.

The sun was flogging the street. Not an animal was stirring. But the townspeople, leaning against the walls of the houses or sitting at the doors and windows, were whispering to one another.

"Aren't these people taking their siesta today?" asked Evaristo Peixoto. He felt uneasy.

The collector spoke softly, as if to himself:

"They're waiting."

Evaristo Peixoto perceived an obscene inflection of fear in the collector's voice. He looked at him disconcertedly.

They arrived at the store. It was closed.

"Didn't we say three o'clock?"

The collector tried to answer in a way that would not anger the revenue agent:

"You said three o'clock, sir. Miguel didn't say anything."

Evaristo Peixoto took out a cigarette and lit it. The collector looked at his companion's hands to see if they were shaking. They were not.

"Mr. Peixoto, I think it's right for me to warn you."

"Warn me about what?"

"About Miguel."

"He's a fool."

"I ought to warn you. He's not such a fool. Miguel is a

strange man. He's sick. Everybody's sick here, haven't you
noticed? Who can stay healthy under this sun. But he's sick in
a different way. Be careful of him."

The revenue agent replied in a loud voice:

"Why, he's nothing but a walking corpse. He doesn't even
have enough strength to come and open this lousy store."

From the hard, metallic blue of the sky, the implacable sun
continued to pour fire on the ruined town. Behind the roofs,
against a desolate background, the obelisks, more like grave-
stones than ever, were aglow.

"Miguel isn't really bad," continued the collector nervously.
"He just won't stand for anyone interfering in his life. And he's
sort of crazy on one subject: he hates revenue agents."

"Oh?"

"I meant to tell you yesterday. I don't know how I forgot.
I warn all the revenue agents who come here. Besides, Miguel
knows accounting. You saw his books, how correctly he keeps
them. You won't find a single mistake. It's best not to do anything more. Put your okeh on his return and forget about it.
That's what all the revenue agents who come here do, although
they know, as I know, as everybody here knows . . ."

The collector looked fearfully around and then continued, almost in a whisper:

"Everybody knows that Miguel has barrels and barrels of rum
with no revenue stamps on them. He keeps them in a storeroom
in the back."

Evaristo Peixoto felt that this was something more than a
warning, something more than the collector's concern for his wel-
fare. He sensed intrigue. He was certain that his companion
wanted to prod him into a confrontation for which he, the collector, lacked the courage.

"I see."

"But I wouldn't investigate him. It isn't worth it. Miguel is a
strange sort. The agents who have come here all agreed with
me. We're far away here. The police, politics, Miguel controls
them. No use challenging him. And with this sun . . . This sun
does everybody in, every living creature. . . ."

The revenue agent took out his handkerchief, wiped his
sweaty face, and looked again at the people who were waiting,

safe, in the shade. He called a small boy, gave him a nickel, and sent him to Miguel's house with a message. The boy ran off. The people now were fluttering like corn tassels in the wind. The boy returned quickly.

"Mr. Miguel says he's not going to open his store any more today."

The revenue agent shouted so that the people could hear him: "This dog will learn that he can't fool around with me."

A new wave of excitement swept through the townspeople. Additional heads appeared at the windows. Murmurs spread. Mothers called to their children to stay close. Steam rose from the hot earth.

"Go and tell that dog that, if he doesn't come, I'll go and get him."

Nervous, sweating, the collector edited the message:

"Ask Mr. Miguel Noronha to do Mr. Peixoto the favor of opening the store, because Mr. Peixoto plans to leave tomorrow."

More waiting under the cruel sun and under the strangely concentrated attention of these subhumans.

This time Miguel complied. With the salesman at his side, he walked slowly, his key ring in his hand, an open parasol over his head. He dragged his feet, making a noise with his wooden slippers on the hard ground. With a barely audible "good afternoon," he opened the door. Evaristo Peixoto noted how calm he was. Not a drop of sweat on the little man's skin, as if he were immune to sun and heat.

Inside the store the books on the counter were just as the revenue agent had left them. He opened them again. He knew it was useless to examine them; he knew he would find no evidence in them of the man's illegal activities. He pretended to work at them, however, while he decided what to do next. He was frowning. He expected Miguel to lie in the hammock, but this time the store owner sat down behind his writing desk, which was located between the counter and the door at the back of the store. The agent breathed deeply as if to control his accelerating pulse. He glanced over his glasses at the withered little man. Miguel's body, now immobile, had dropped to one side as if he lacked the energy to sit erect. His bulging, yellow eyes, although fixed on Evaristo Peixoto, were expressionless. The agent shut the last book. Slowly he took off his glasses, put them in their case, and put the case in his pocket. Silent, intense, he faced the store owner. After a few moments the agent spoke:

"Your books are in order."

"I know that," replied Miguel.

There was a long pause. The silence was so oppressive that everyone felt it physically.

"However, I'll have to examine your merchandise."

Miguel did not bat an eye.

"If my books are in order, you have no right to meddle in anything else."

"I'll have to examine your merchandise," repeated the agent, as if he had not heard Miguel.

"I know you have illegal merchandise hidden in your storeroom," he said coolly. "Rum. It has no revenue stamps. And I'm going to report it."

The store owner said nothing. The collector tried to intervene: "Don't . . ."

The agent pushed him aside and addressed Miguel again:

"I'm going to take a look at your barrels of rum."

"No revenue agent has ever gone behind this counter," said the withered little man. "And no revenue agent ever will."

Evaristo Peixoto turned toward the collector.

"Go call the mayor."

The collector went out. Neither the revenue agent nor the store owner moved. The collector returned.

"The mayor isn't there. He left town this morning on a trip."

"Then call the chief of police."

"He left too . . . this morning."

Evaristo Peixoto breathed deeply.

"Bring the deputy."

"He left at noon to go to his farm. Don't you see, it's useless to press the matter. We're too far away. . . . And with this sun . . ."

The revenue agent exploded:

"Shut up, coward. You're going to be fired. What kind of a tax collector are you, letting this man cheat the government. Go get two witnesses."

"No one will come."

Outside, the people clustered in what little shade they could find. They were afraid to come very close. Evaristo Peixoto knew what they were waiting for, the degenerates.

The sun beat ferociously on the street and on the scorched roofs.

The faint sound of a drawer opening alerted the revenue agent. The collector slinked away from him. The salesman scurried to a corner. The agent felt completely alone. Miguel's hands, which had been resting on the desk, were no longer visible. A chill ran down Evaristo Peixoto's spine.

"I'll have to examine your merchandise," he said, as if this were the burden of a song—a dirge.

The store owner did not reply. Evaristo Peixoto was sweating from every pore. Sweat bathed his forehead and his bald head, soaked his collar, glued his shirt to his body. His tongue swelled with the bitter taste of bile. His stomach contracted. Gently he slid his hand down into his trouser pocket. In his soft fingers appeared a little Mauser, its trigger cocked.

"I'll have to examine your merchandise." Despite everything, his voice was firm.

The withered little man, still sitting drooped to one side behind the desk, did not move. The revenue agent advanced. The pounding of his blood deafened him. His awareness of his surroundings, his consciousness of what he had come there to do and of the action he had decided to take, became a vague jumble in his mind. All that he saw clearly were two bulging eyes staring at him. He wanted to vault over the counter but his legs would not let him. His finger on the trigger felt paralyzed. His arm was slowly sinking to his side. He heard the sound of the drawer as it closed. He turned his back to the withered little man and left the store. In the street he walked slowly past the gaze of the townspeople and he knew that he was one of them—miserably, horribly, one of them.

* * *

CARLOS VASCONCELOS MAIA was born in 1923 in Santa Inês, Bahia. When he was a child, his family moved to Salvador, the state capital, where he still lives.

He has been, among other things, a sports reporter, a merchant, and a stock and insurance broker. "Sun" ("Sol"), from *O Cavalo e a Rosa,* 1955, is one of the fruits of his trips through the interior of Bahia as a traveling salesman. From 1959 to 1964 he served the city of Salvador as Director of Tourism, a subject on which he remains a prominent consultant.

Vasconcelos Maia's writings include newspaper columns, novellas, and several books of short stories. He is represented in eight short-story anthologies.